I BOUGHT EVERY DREAM
HE SOLD ME 2

J. DOMINIQUE

I Bought Every Dream He Sold Me 2

Copyright © 2022 by J. Dominique

All rights reserved.

Published in the United States of America.

Published by Cole Hart Signature, LLC.

Mailing List

To stay up to date on new releases, plus get information on contests, sneak peeks, and more,

Go To The Website Below...

www.colehartsignature.com

PREVIOUSLY
QUAY

It was finally the day I'd been waiting on, and knowing I was going to kill Bronx's ass had me in a good ass mood. It had taken every bit of restraint I had not to go behind Heavy's back and just snatch that nigga out his bed in the middle of the night and put a bullet between his eyes. I tried to keep myself busy trying to get back in Isis's good graces, but since she wasn't fucking with me like that, I still ended up with a lot of free time on my hands. If I wasn't blowing bags on her ass and trying to pop up on her then I was working out, as much as I could with my injuries anyway. It had only been a few weeks since I'd left the hospital but I felt like I was in good enough shape for the task at hand. Since I was trying to do real damage, I was preparing my Kel-Tec P50 with two extra drums. It was my favorite gun and I couldn't wait to use it.

"Bro, not the lil' handheld joint with drums!" Manny clowned me as soon as I got in the car with his stupid ass. He sat behind the wheel with a Mack 10 in his lap and a blunt dangling from his lips. Frowning, I instantly snatched that shit away and took a couple pulls before tossing it out the window. "Man, what the fuck you doin'!"

"Nigga, we ridin' with guns and shit, yo' goofy ass can't be smokin'! Fuck wrong with you!" I snapped, unfazed by the nasty look he was giving me even though he knew I was right. "Move this raggedy piece of shit, we still gotta pick up Heavy." The mention of Heavy had his face growing tighter.

"You was serious about that shit?" he questioned. "I thought for sure yo' ass was playin', bro. How you figure you can even trust his ass?" I couldn't front, I had gone back and forth about whether or not I really wanted to let Heavy bust this move with us. Knowing that he was a real one had played a major role in the decision though. He'd held off on killing that nigga after the disloyal shit he'd pulled and I had to respect it. Plus, he'd been trying to put his bid in with Adore and I had to admit they were a good look. Especially considering what type of goofy ass baby daddy she had. My sister needed a nigga that was about his business and would fuck a nigga or bitch up behind her. I was hoping at some point he'd beat that nigga's ass and tag me the fuck in.

"Naw, bro good. Besides, he damn near bouta be my brother-in-law, so you might as well get used to him being around," I told him, leaning back in my seat with a shrug. That nigga's head looked like it was about to explode.

"I thought you said she wasn't fuckin' with nobody! You know I was tryna get yo' sister pregnant, nigga!" I shot a warning look at his ass, only for him to buck his eyes at me. "Don't be lookin' at me like that muhfucka, you knew I wanted Adore!"

"My sister don't want yo' Kodak Black lookin' ass! Stop playin' and let's go, ole goofy ass nigga!"

"Aye man, fuck you, I don't look like that nigga!" he huffed, begrudgingly dropping the car into drive and pulling off. That nigga knew damn well I ain't play about my sister, so it went without saying that I'd never let her fuck with a nigga like him. Niko had slipped through the cracks because I was young and doing *my own thing, but now I was a grown ass man and wasn't at all ashamed to say I'd cockblock like a muthafucka.*

After telling him where to go to pick up Heavy, Manny's crybaby ass cut the radio up and drove in silence, stewing over the insult or Adore, probably both. I shot a text to Heavy to let him know we were on the way, and then I somehow ended up in Isis and my message thread. She'd been giving me dry ass replies any time I texted her, but at least she was still messaging me back. I quickly asked if she wanted me to bring her some food, knowing that was the key to shorty's heart. She was already greedy as fuck, so I could only imagine how much worse it was going to get with my baby in her stomach. I smirked when my phone vibrated a second later with her response, giving me a long list of shit she wanted, and I let her know I'd be there soon before shoving my phone back into my pocket. Hopefully, I'd be able to bring her food and slide into some pussy after she was well fed and in a good mood.

We pulled up outside of Pam's restaurant and before the car could stop all the way, Heavy came swaggering out. He squinted at the raggedy ass car but ducked into the back seat once he saw me.

"What's up, big homie?" I turned around and bumped fists with him. "You know Manny, right?"

"Yeah, what's up," he said, nodding, only to get a grunt out of Manny's ass. Heavy either didn't notice or just didn't give a fuck about that nigga's dry ass response as he settled into the back seat. Since Manny was acting like a little bitch, I decided to fuck with him further.

"Aye, you talked to Adore today?" I quizzed, looking at Manny with a smirk, and he sucked his teeth but kept his eyes on the road.

"Yeah, she's back at the restaurant. My OG tryna convince her to sell her cakes in there and shit."

"Oh, that's what's up. Adore can bake her ass off for real. Them muhfuckas definitely gone sell out." I nodded, hoping she'd agree to do it, especially if it was going to put more money in her pockets. She

was still thinking that Niko would look out and honor their original agreement, but even I knew that shit wasn't happening. That contract had her boxed into a corner and if she didn't make the type of money they were talking about in there, then I had no doubt they'd try to take my niece away forever. If it came to that then I'd definitely dead all them muthafuckas and not feel guilty about it in the slightest.

Noticing that we'd made it to that nigga's neighborhood had me perking up in my seat, more than ready to get this shit over with. I made sure the safety was off my gun as we parked on the street and scoped out the house. Heavy had already checked in to make sure that nigga was home, and the lights clicking on from the inside let me know it was true. We waited a few minutes before making our way on foot across his lawn, staying along the tall ass shrubs so as not to be detected. I was surprised his ass didn't have flood lights out there, but then again, the type of nigga Bronx was, he probably didn't think anybody was bold enough to come to his crib. Unfortunately for him, I was a bold muthafucka and had no problem maneuvering toward his house. We were halfway around the huge ass yard when a car came whipping into his driveway, damn near running into one of the three cars he had parked out there. I immediately ducked behind the bush closest to me and so did Heavy and Manny. Our dark clothes made it easy to blend into the night, but the lack of lighting in his yard made it almost impossible to see whoever it was that had pulled up. I could barely make out the dark ass car as the person leaned into the back seat and pulled out a huge garbage bag. Squinting, I was able to tell it was a woman and even though I didn't try to harm females, this particular one was just going to be at the wrong place at the wrong time. She struggled up to the door with the bag like it was heavy as hell and instantly started knocking and ringing the bell like her ass was crazy, while I prepared to pounce as soon as the door was opened.

"Aye, what the fuck you doin' all that shit for?" Bronx's voice

was barely audible from where I was crouched at, and I moved closer so I wouldn't have too far to go when I decided to rush him.

"I'm bringin' you yo' shit! I'm not fuckin' with you so stop sendin' shit to me!" she screamed, and I could hear that nigga laughing at her ass, but I was stuck on the sound of her voice. I knew that shit well because she'd been going off on my ass a lot recently. My neck shot out so I could get a better view, and I was shocked to see Isis standing there clowning. I didn't even think before I was storming the short distance to where they stood while Manny called out to me. The look on her and Bronx's face was priceless as I stepped up and placed my gun to her head.

"You got some fuckin' explainin' to do, baby mama."

CHAPTER ONE

ISIS

My mouth instantly went dry as Quay pressed the cold barrel to my head, glaring at me sinisterly. With wide eyes, I watched two other niggas dressed in black rush Bronx and begin beating his ass. The situation coupled with the look in Quay's eyes had me trembling and unable to stop the trickle of pee from pooling in my sweats. He'd never looked at me with so much malice in his eyes, and I just knew I was about to die.

"Qu-Quay, what are y-you doing?" I stuttered, afraid to move or even breath too hard.

"Naw, what the fuck are *you* doin'? How you even know this nigga?" He took the gun off of me long enough to point it at Bronx's limp body, and I caught a glimpse of the drums attached to it, before he brought it back my way. Stunned, I threw my hands up in front of me.

"We te-texted for a while." I knew the answer sounded lame coming out, but I honestly didn't know how else to explain it. I never thought Quay would be following me and go this far after we'd stopped fucking around, considering all the bitches he'd messed with. There was no way he'd brought his ass over there to attack his competitor and hold me at gunpoint. Not when he'd just been living his life and fucking whoever he wanted. I hadn't even let Bronx anywhere near my pussy and he was ready to murder my black ass. As mad as I was though, I wasn't stupid enough to say any of that out loud, not while he had that gun anyway.

My response only had his eyes growing darker, and he mushed the gun harder against my temple as he leaned down into my face. "How the fuck you know where he live then, huh? What's in them bags? That's some shit he bought you?" He was going off and raising his voice with each question, finally drawing the attention of the niggas he'd come with.

"Aye man, chill the fuck out! This ain't no time for a domestic shit!" My eyes ballooned seeing Heavy step up. "Let her go," he said much more calmly but with a level of authority that had him and Quay in a standoff. The third nigga, who I now recognized as Manny, looked at them irritably and scoffed as he stood.

"I'm bouta go grab the car. Y'all muhfuckas better have this shit figured out by the time I get back." He walked off grumbling while they continued to stare each other down before Quay slowly dropped his arm. As soon as the weapon was no longer on me, I hauled off and slapped the dog shit out of him. Dropping his chin, he prepared to charge me, but Heavy jumped between us.

"Fuck you, Ja'Quay! You pointing guns at me and shit now? It's fuck me and this baby all of a sudden, you piece of shit!" I screamed, feeling much braver since there was distance and a buff ass nigga in between us. I fought to get to him, as their car pulled up behind mine and Manny jumped out, shaking his head at the scene before him.

"You lucky I ain't splatter yo' fuckin' brains on this asphalt!

You out here fuckin' with the nigga that tried to take me out? You at my fuckin' opp's house? Hell yeah, it's fuck you, bitch!" He started back toward me only to be pushed away by Manny. My mouth instantly snapped closed as his words hit me. I was confused as fuck and trying to piece together how out of all the niggas in Chicago, I'd stumbled upon the one that tried to kill my baby daddy.

"Wh-what?" I panted, unable to catch my breath as I looked from him to Bronx in disbelief. "What are you talking about? I—"

"Take yo' ass home, bro," he growled lowly, not even looking at me as he spoke.

"But—"

"On my soul, I already wanna kill yo' ass. Go the fuck home before I bury you with this nigga." His voice was eerily calm as he set his cold eyes on me, and a shiver went down my spine. I'd never been afraid of Quay, not even when he was the most pissed off he'd ever been, but at the moment I was scared shitless.

"Aye, yo' ass tweakin' for real. Go over there and help him get that nigga in the trunk, I got her."

Heavy turned slightly and gave Quay a stern look that had him eventually walking off with Manny to where Bronx still lay in his doorway. Giving me an apologetic expression, he guided me to my car, silently waiting as I slid behind the wheel on shaky legs and put on my seatbelt. My hands were trembling so bad that it took me way longer than it should have just to get it to latch. As scared as I was, I still paused to look for Quay in my rearview before finally speeding out of the driveway. The trip home was full of questions as I went back through every encounter I'd had with Bronx. Did he know the whole time that I had a connection to Quay? There wasn't anything strange about the way we met or any of the conversations we'd had and it never got too deep, and after the shit with that crazy ass girl, I'd put an end to whatever it was we had going on.

Even after I blocked him though, he was sending me shit to my store since he didn't know where I lived. With him and Quay both sending me things I quickly got fed up, and while I had no choice but to deal with my baby daddy, I refused to put up with Bronx's harassment too. So I bagged up everything he'd sent, which were flowers, stuffed animals, and even a couple of bags, so I could just drop it off to him and let his ass know to leave me alone. The very last thing I was expecting was for Quay to pop up out of nowhere and point a fucking gun at me. I was still in disbelief almost an hour later when I parked in front of my apartment, and I was suddenly feeling sick. Would Quay really have done any of the shit he'd claimed he would? Was it even safe to be home when he finally finished whatever he was doing to Bronx?

I looked around nervously like his ass would pop out of the bushes again, before taking a deep breath and climbing out of my car. As soon as I did, I got dizzy as fuck, my stomach turned violently, and I threw up everything in my stomach.

"Ewww bitch, you okay?" I looked up to see my neighbor Carmise watching me from her porch with her face scrunched up. Wiping my mouth with the back of my hand, I nodded, unsure of whether or not it was the baby or my nerves that had me out there vomiting. "Damn, you sure?"

"I said I'm fine!" I snapped nastily, pushing myself off my car and willing my wobbly legs to move. She instantly began talking shit, but I ignored her and focused only on getting myself inside. After the night I'd had, I didn't have time to deal with her ass. Behind the safety of my four walls, I locked both the knob and the top lock before going around to check the others. Once I'd finished, I scoffed at myself, realizing Quay still had my damn keys and could literally come and go whenever he wanted. I contemplated going to Ms. Deb's house just in case his crazy ass did decide to come, but I was too embarrassed. My mama's house was completely out of the question too because she'd ask too many questions. Besides, Quay was crazy enough to show up there too, and since he didn't like my mama he'd fuck around and hold her at gunpoint too.

In an attempt to stop my brain from racing, I closed my eyes and took a couple of calming breaths. I was really overthinking this shit and once Quay calmed down I'd explain to him that I didn't know shit about him and Bronx's beef. Obviously he wanted to have a conversation or he wouldn't have let me go. He could've easily put my ass in the trunk or shot me on the spot, but he didn't and that gave me a little bit of hope we could get through this without me ending up dead.

Even with that thought in mind I still couldn't relax. I started to pour me a drink to calm my nerves and remembered that my ass couldn't drink, so instead, I decided on a warm bath. Working on autopilot, I poured all my usual self-care products into the running water and lit a few candles. The bathroom instantly became overpowered with the smell of lavender and I took deep breaths as I stripped down to nothing before climbing into the soothing water. Closing my eyes, I let my head rest against the small pillow I had set up on the back of my tub, but I wasn't even able to do that for long. Thoughts of Quay's threats had me constantly peeking out of one eye in fear that he'd creep in and be standing over me like a crazy person. After the fifth time, I realized a bath wasn't going to do shit to calm my nerves. Frustrated, I hurriedly washed up a few times before rinsing my body and wrapping one of my plush cream towels around myself. Next I brushed my teeth, swishing twice with Listerine just to make sure my mouth was extra clean after the way I threw up.

I felt completely drained as I padded into my room, and

instead of going through my normal moisturizing routine I climbed into bed with the towel still wrapped around me. I laid there restlessly as the initial fear faded and was quickly replaced with hurt. My own child's father held me at gunpoint and threatened to kill me because he thought I was somehow in cahoots with his enemy. An enemy I'd unwittingly been seeing in an effort to get over his ass. And speaking of Bronx, I couldn't help wondering if he had intentionally sought me out in some type of dick swinging contest he was having with Quay. If that was the case, then not only did I have his delusional hoes to worry about, I also had his enemies coming after me too. Every time I turned around there were signs telling me I should leave his ass alone. Between the shit with Bronx and then the way Quay acted back at his house, I was even more inclined to put distance between us. I just hoped our baby was enough to keep him from hurting me.

CHAPTER TWO

QUAY

"Wake yo' bitch ass up, nigga!" I growled, backhanding Bronx out of the stupor Heavy had put him in. His head slammed into his shoulder from the rough blow and Manny hissed behind me.

"God damn, A Pimp Named Slick Back! Yo' ass almost just broke that nigga neck with that slap! I know that shit hurt!" I didn't even turn around to acknowledge his goofy ass comment. Instead, I kept my steely gaze on Bronx as he glared at me hatefully. I'd been waiting to get him to Heavy's warehouse so I could beat the Isis out his ass. Even though I didn't know how deep shit had gotten between him and my baby mama, knowing that he had any dealings with her had me seeing red. I was so mad I said and did shit to Isis that I wouldn't have dared to before. It was like I couldn't control myself though, and not even the look of hurt that crossed her face was enough to squelch my rage. Despite what I'd said, she was lucky she brought up our baby, or else her ass was gonna be right in the trunk along with that nigga. Just thinking of how close I'd come to killing my flesh and blood had me sending a flurry of blows to his face. Blood instantly squirted from his nose and mouth, only fueling my anger even more.

"Aye, give me that machete." I stepped back and held my hand out.

"Aw hell naw, bro! I ain't fuckin' with it! Shoot that nigga or break his neck or some shit, I ain't tryna watch you chop his ass up!" Manny immediately refused. Sighing, I tore my eyes away from the bloody mess in front of me to glare his way, but he only looked back at me unfazed. The stare off was interrupted by the sound of laughter coming from behind me.

"These the muhfuckas you rollin' with now, bro?" Bronx directed to Heavy, laughing until it turned into a fit of coughing.

"Better them than a nigga who'd steal from me and fuck my baby mama." Heavy shrugged like he hadn't just said an earful.

"Damn, this nigga just goin' around fuckin' everybody baby mama," Manny's dumb ass huffed, shaking his head in disbelief. I couldn't lie, even I was surprised to hear Heavy divulge some shit like that, but I wasn't going to speak on it.

"That's *our* baby mama, goofy ass nigga! You sound 'bout dumb as his ass!" Bronx spat, tossing his head in my direction. "I been fuckin' shorty since high school. You thought you popped that cherry? Ha! Thirsty ass bitch only fucked with you 'cause yo' pockets were fatter, but I broke that pussy in. Shit, Kay Kay might be mine I was bussin' in that bitch so much—"

Heavy had been silently taking in everything he said until the mention of his daughter. I didn't blame him one bit when he shot over to that nigga and went across his shit before tucking the gun under his chin.

"Keep my baby name out yo' fuckin' mouth, pussy ass nigga!" His finger tightened on the trigger and I could tell it was taking everything in him not to pull that shit. Shaking with rage, he shoved the gun deeper into his neck as he smirked sinisterly. Even though he'd basically asked for this by running his mouth, the look of fear in Bronx's eyes was unmistakable. I guess he figured he could stall for time with his little villain speech, but Heavy was ready to blow his brains out the top of his head. Not wanting to miss the opportunity for one of my bullets to be the fatal one, I drew mine gun as well, placing it at his chest, right over his heart.

"You bouta shoot me over a hoe and a lil' bit of money?" Bronx asked through clenched teeth, giving Heavy a hard stare.

"Nah, I'm bouta *kill* yo' ass 'cause you're a grimy ass nigga and I can't trust you. Once a snake, always a snake." This shit was turning real soap opera-ish, and I was just ready to bury his ass. I cracked my neck and flexed my fingers around my gun's handle since I was holding it so tight my shit ached.

"Ayite, kiss my babies for me," he hinted, turning his gaze on me with a bloody grin. No longer waiting on Heavy, I began unloading my clip in his chest, making his body jerk long after the light left his eyes. I didn't even stop once I realized he was dead. It wasn't until Heavy put a hand over my forearm that I finally released the trigger and snatched away. As crazy as it sounded, I was more pissed off about the possibility that the baby Isis was pregnant with could be his than I was about that nigga trying to kill me. Being a street nigga, I knew there was a high risk of me dying every time I stepped out the door, so beef and bullets came with the territory. Having my girl fucking my enemy behind my back though, that was something completely different and it was damn sure not some shit I was expecting.

"I know damn well he wasn't tryna say both y'all's niggas shorties is his? Maaaaan, I'd be ready to kill a bitch 'bout playin' with me like that," Manny griped, sucking his teeth. He quickly piped down though when Heavy shot a look his way while I paced and tried to calm myself down.

"Don't listen to his ass. Niggas will say anything when they know they're bouta die. He was obviously using the people we care most about to fuck with us." His words stopped me in my tracks and my eyes narrowed to slits.

"I ain't tryna hear that shit right now, bro. She was at that nigga crib, and you said it yourself that he been fuckin' yo' baby mama, so what the fuck I'm s'posed to think? You tryna tell me his little speech ain't got you questioning shit?" I asked, even though I didn't really want to know. If I was being honest, I didn't even want to be having the conversation at all, but it was the only thing keeping me from pulling up on Ice with another full clip. Heavy's jaw flexed as he looked off, giving away just how disturbed he really was about the shit that nigga said. He could talk all the shit he wanted to, but there was no avoiding the implications.

"Exactly!" I spat, feeling vindicated. I turned my back on him, only growing more enraged by the confirmation.

"Don't let the words of a dead nigga make you do some shit you gone regret," he said before I ducked out the door. I shrugged his words off though, too pissed to even let them sink in and stop me from what I was about to do.

A couple hours later, I sat with my gun on my lap as I watched Isis sleep. The tiny sliver of moonlight illuminated off her smooth skin, and I found myself admiring her beauty despite my sinister thoughts. She'd been tossing and turning since I'd gotten there, making her towel fall off to expose her succulent body. My jaw clenched as she released a whimper that sounded way too sensual for the distress on her face. I leaned closer, trying to decipher whatever it was she was mumbling.

"No, no, please," she moaned, shaking her head from side to side. "*Baby*, don't!"

My reasonable side was telling me she was upset, more than likely from me pulling a gun on her ass earlier, but the more irrational side of me wondered if she was dreaming about that nigga. It was crazy as hell, but after the shit Bronx revealed I couldn't help but think the worst.

The hold on my gun tightened at the thought just as her eyes popped open and she inhaled a sharp breath at the sight of me. I remained silent, surprised that she didn't immediately scream when she sat up and pulled the towel back around herself.

"Q-Quay," she stammered, moving to create some distance between us. I was completely unmoved by the fear on her face as her eyes lowered to the gun in my lap.

"Is that that nigga's baby?" The way her brows shot up let me know that was the last thing she expected to come out my mouth, but anger quickly replaced her look of shock.

"Oh, you done really lost yo' black ass mind," she huffed, climbing to her knees. "Get the fuck out my house, Ja'Quay!" I stood up slowly, gripping my gun in my right hand.

"The slim chance that might be my baby is the only thing saving yo' ass right now, on my soul. Stay yo' hoe ass from around me until we can get a blood test, bro."

"Ughhhh, fuck you! Fuck you!" she shouted at my back, even going so far as to throw a pillow at me as I left the room. I hated that I even had to question whether or not I'd planted that seed in her, but I damn sure wasn't about to take the implication lightly. Ignoring her continued screams, I stepped out onto the porch, not at all surprised to see her nosy ass neighbor still out on her own stoop smoking a wood. My bruised pride led me over there when I should've been taking my ass home, but it was already too late. Not even ten minutes later, I stood in her living room fucking her face. Even as I sent my kids down her throat though, it was Isis's tear-streaked face that invaded my mind.

CHAPTER THREE

ADORE

I frowned as another one of my calls to Isis went unanswered. It wasn't like her to go MIA on me, and I couldn't help but be a little worried. I shot her a quick text, knowing it probably wouldn't get a response either, and made a mental note to drop in on her later. Her little disappearing act couldn't have come at a worst time since I was already on edge about my interview with Abby Shaw. After hearing the little bit of my story she was excited as hell to meet with me and get the dirt on the Black family. She wanted to write the piece first before bringing it to the attention of her boss, but she'd already let me know it was definitely some front page news. That had me both geeked and nervous at the same time. As bad as I wanted to tell my side of the story and put my baby daddy's family on blast, I was a little worried about what they'd do once they found out. Still, I wasn't worried enough not to go through with it though.

"Adore, you got a new group in your section," Felicia called out, rolling her eyes and pointing to a booth that was occupied by a frazzled looking woman and four rowdy ass kids. Instead of flipping her off like I wanted to, I put on a stiff smile and headed over to their table, making sure to grab a couple coloring sheets and crayons on the way.

Despite how hyper the kids were, they surprisingly settled down once they each had a paper in front of them and I was able to take down their orders with no problem. The rest of my shift pretty much went the same way, with Felicia's irritating ass sending the hardest customers to my section and me still managing to get the job done.

By the end of my shift I was exhausted and my feet were killing me, but I'd already been penciled into Abby's tight schedule, so once I counted out my tips I scheduled an Uber. It probably would've made sense to have her just meet me at Pam's, but the last thing I wanted was any of the messy bitches that worked with me in my business. They were already acting funny because of Heavy, I didn't need any of them finding out about Niko or our daughter. At least not yet anyway.

It wasn't long before I was pulling up at home, and I rushed to shower and change into some sweats before Abby arrived. The hot water and soft fabric felt wonderful and if it wasn't for her knocking as soon as I came back downstairs, I probably would've been curled up sleeping.

"Hey, Adore?"

"Abby?" we both asked at the same time, chuckling at how in sync it was.

"That's me, come on in." I opened the door wider and stepped aside to let her in after we shook hands. "Would you like something to drink or anything?" My hospitality kicked right in and I laughed nervously at how much I sounded like a waitress.

"Actually, a bottle of water would be great." She smiled, getting comfortable on the couch. I hurried off to fulfill her request, and while I was in the kitchen I took a minute to get myself together. Abby was the first person who wanted anything to do with my troubles after finding out the Black family was involved. It was like they had the whole city in their pockets, so to finally have somebody willing to listen had me feeling pressured to not scare her off. Taking a deep breath, I grabbed two water bottles from the fridge and rejoined Abby in the living room.

"I hope Aquafina is okay."

"Oh yeah, Aquafina is cool." She took a quick sip and set hers on the table as I took a seat across from her.

"I, um, I really don't know how this is supposed to go. I never talked about this with anybody so I'm not sure where to start." My voice trailed off and she gave me an encouraging smile.

"Why don't you just start from the beginning and try to be as forthcoming as you can," she coached, pulling a small tape recorder out of her bag along with a pen and pad. "I may interject if I need clarification, but other than that, just tell your story."

With a nod, I began telling her everything, starting from the moment I met Niko all the way to our last conversation. True to her word she listened well, only interrupting to ask a question here and there. She even wrote down some notes and by the time I finished, her face was covered in sympathy.

"Damn, I knew the Blacks were crooked but letting you go down for an accident that was self-defense at best and then snatching your baby? Not to mention Niko being an obvious predator. That's a lot, I don't even know how you haven't lost your mind, girl." Shaking her head, she looked down at her notes and scoffed.

"I mean, my family has been very supportive and always had my back so they keep me sane, but it is hard not being able to see Kaliyah, or finding a lawyer willing to go against Niko and his daddy. There have been plenty of times I wanted to give up but I just can't, not until I'm able to have a relationship with my baby." I didn't realize I was crying until I felt a tear land on my arm. I quickly wiped my face as Abby held out some Kleenex to me.

"And you definitely deserve that plus some after all you've been through," she said, giving my hand a squeeze. "I won't lie, I wasn't sure about where this story was going. At best I thought it was some kind of scandal or super risqué gossip, but *this*. This is so much more. People need to know what type of family they're supporting and Kaliyah needs to know her real mother." It felt good to have someone outside of my immediate circle finally hear me out and before I could stop myself, I pulled her into a hug as more tears flowed down my face.

"Thank you so much! You don't know how much it means to hear that." I sniffled.

"You don't have to thank me. Anybody with a heart would say the same thing," she told me, patting my back soothingly. As encouraging as her words were, I couldn't help feeling slightly embarrassed after a minute of hugging a complete stranger, and I finally released her from my hold. Chuckling awkwardly, I wiped my face, avoiding eye contact.

"Sorry about that, I'm usually better at keeping my emotions in check."

"Girl, you're cool. Sometimes we just need to cry it out, especially with the way the odds are stacked up against us. As long as when you finish you clean your face and readjust your crown, 'cause you can't let these niggas see you sweat." She smirked to lighten the mood. "Now, I think that what we have here is a good foundation for you to shake up Niko and his family. I'll compile all of this and present it to my boss, and I should be able to let you know by the end of the week when we'll run the story." She cut the recorder and tossed it back into her bag along with her pen and paper. Suddenly, I was nervous all over again hearing about the wait I'd have to endure. No doubt I'd be on pins and needles until I heard back from her, but at least I'd made a step in the right direction.

"Okay, and thanks again for helping me get the truth out. I know you're taking a big risk writing something like this Abby—"

"Oh, you can just call me Meka," she cut me off with a chuckle as I walked her to the door. "I use Abby as my professional name so people will take my writing more seriously." She used air quotes with a roll of her eyes. I had to admit, Meka definitely fit her better.

"I feel that." I nodded. "Well, thanks *Meka*, I really do appreciate this."

"No need to thank me, this has been a long time coming." With that she was gone. I watched as she climbed into her car and pulled off, sending a quick prayer up that everything worked out. In an effort to shake the anxious feeling creeping up my neck, I decided to go and check on Isis like I'd planned. I took a chance and called her again, only for it to ring until her voicemail picked up. Preparing to try again, I was surprised when a text came through, and my brows immediately bunched.

Bestie: Sorry boo, I've been sleeping all day *eye roll emoji* I think I got some type of stomach virus but I'll be good in a couple days.

Obviously she thought that vague ass text would be enough to calm my concern, but she should've known me better than that. I probably would've believed it if she wasn't ducking my calls, so I dialed her right back up and she picked up right before the voicemail would've.

"Ughhh, yes mother?" she answered smartly, and I could imagine her rolling her eyes in annoyance.

"Not you havin' an attitude 'cause I'm calling to check on you, heffa." My tone was teasing even though I was really tempted to FaceTime her ass so I could lay eyes on her. She didn't sound like her usual self, but I guessed sleeping all day in between vomiting would make anyone's voice be a little off. Still, I couldn't help thinking it was something else going on.

"No bestie, I don't have an attitude, but my throat is sore as fuck from throwing up so, I wasn't really trying to talk. That's why I sent yo' ass a text that obviously didn't do the trick, *trick*."

"Well excuse me for being worried about yo' mean ass. I'm gone blame this feistiness on yo' empty stomach, so I'll bring you some soup from Panera. You're clearly not yourself when you're hungry." I was already slipping on my UGGs as I spoke.

"No, you don't have to do all that, girl. I can't stomach anything besides crackers right now anyway," she interjected, and I paused in the middle of putting on my hoodie with a frown. "Ugh, hold on—" I heard her gag, and then begin moving around before the sound of her retching filled my ears, almost making me throw up myself.

"Oh damn, you sure you don't need to go to the hospital or something?" I asked when she finally came back on the line panting. It was weird to hear her sound so bad considering how upbeat she usually was, and it only made me feel worse for her.

"I already did, that's how I know it's a virus. It's just gonna have to run its course. I'll be fine though, I'ma sleep this shit off and be good as new in a couple days." As bad as I wanted to fight her on it, I decided to not push. She was already not feeling well and I didn't want to make her stay on the phone if it hurt to even talk.

"Ayite boo, just keep me updated. At least shoot me a text

to let me know you're good," I ordered, fully intending to pull up on her if she disappeared again.

"Ok, I promise I'll check in, mama," she teased, beginning to shuffle around again. "I'm bouta brush my teeth and lay back down for a few though." Satisfied with her response, I finally let her off the phone so she could handle her business and made a mental note to also have Quay drop by on her. I knew she'd probably be more willing to let her boo come over and baby her than me, regardless of what her mouth said.

CHAPTER FOUR

HEAVY

It had been a couple of days since we got rid of that nigga Bronx and despite the shit I'd been talking to Quay, I was still fucked up behind the things he'd said. I'd been up every night since, studying Kay Kay's pictures to see if there was any type of resemblance between her and him. His words were haunting me so bad I had to go MIA on Sha'ron and my baby. I already felt like a deadbeat for even letting his words get to me, but it was only made worse by me not being able to look Kay Kay in the face. I kept telling myself my distance was to keep from killing my baby mama but deep down, I knew it was because I had doubts and was feeling guilty about them.

"Yep, just as I suspected. Something's definitely wrong." My mama came into my living room with a look of concern on her face. I'd been so deep in my thoughts I hadn't heard her come in or disable the alarm, which meant that this shit was doing more than making me question my kid. It also had me completely off my square. She dropped her things into a chair and came over, pressing her palm across my forehead like I was a little ass boy.

"What you on, Pamela? I ain't sick," I scoffed, slipping out from under her cool hand and leaning to the the side so I could continue to watch TV, but the sound of her government name coming from my lips instantly had her smacking me upside the head.

"First of all, it's Mama to you, and second of all, you must be sick 'cause me or yo' baby mama ain't seen or heard from you in days." She moved to block my view of the TV with her hands planted on her hips. All traces of concern gone. As bad as I wanted to lie my way out of this shit, my face tightened at the mention of Sha'ron's hoe ass and my mama picked right up on it.

"What that girl done did now that got you so tight, Dominique? You know, I usually stay out y'all business, but it gotta be bad if she calling me 'cause you done disappeared on her." I rubbed the spot she'd hit me in and tried not to explode at the pure audacity of that bitch. She'd been creeping around with my right hand up until a couple of days before but had called my OG because I wasn't readily available to her. As pissed off as I was, she was lucky I wasn't trying to bury her right along with her nigga. "Oh damn, it's that bad?" my OG gasped, seeing my emotions play out on my face, and eased into the spot next to me.

"Shiiit, it's worse," I admitted. "She been fuckin' around with Bronx this whole damn time and... Kay Kay might be his." I damn near choked on the words as I said them and just like I expected, my mama instantly snapped.

"Oh hell naw!" She popped right back up. "That dirty lil' wench! I oughta go beat her ass right now! And Bernard, don't even get me started on his grimy ass! Do they know that you know? Tuh, of course they don't, or else she wouldn't have had the nerve to call me," she answered her own question as she paced angrily.

"Calm down Ma—"

"*Calm down*? How I'm s'posed to do that when muhfuckas out here playing in our faces!" She frowned, suddenly stopping in the middle of the floor, and I shrugged.

"Only one muhfucka playin' in our faces now," I said matter-of-factly, and her brows dipped slightly before understanding covered her face. Usually, I would never let anything like that slip, but the bottle of D'ussé I'd finished had my tongue loose as hell.

"Ooookaay, well I'm gonna act like you didn't just say *that*," she dragged. "What I will say is, I hope you're not planning to take this out on my grandbaby. It's not her fault her mama's a hoe, and whether you take a test or not that's still yo' baby at the end of the day." I wasn't trying to disrespect my OG, but I also wasn't in the mood to hear what she was saying. Not at the moment anyway. It went without saying that regardless of what happened I was the only father Kay Kay knew, and I wasn't going to be the one to break her heart by telling her anything different. I just needed a minute to get my head wrapped around the betrayal and anger I felt from it. If I didn't, I'd fuck around and kill Sha'ron, and regardless of her hoe tendencies she was still a good mother and Kay Kay loved her dumb ass. Tossing my head back on the couch, I let out an irritable groan.

"Ayite, Ma," I told her, hoping she'd accept that answer and leave, but I could still feel her presence looming over me.

"Don't ayite Ma me. You might be going through it right now but what you not gone do is play with Kaylani Giselle Stone. You've been a constant in that girl's life since day one, and I'm gonna expect you to get yourself together and pick up where you left off starting tomorrow, since it's obvious you done had a few," she ordered, sucking her teeth. With a wave of her hand she grabbed her stuff and exited, still talking shit under her breath. She'd left me with a lot to think about. Mainly if I was going to continue on like I didn't know about Sha'ron's bullshit or if I was going to get a DNA test.

———————

Despite a minor hangover I was feeling decent enough to get my ass up and show face at Sha'ron's crib the next morning. Since I called beforehand, my baby girl was already in the window waiting as I pulled up. I barely made it up the stairs before she ran out with a wide smile, and I noticed a gap in her top row of teeth that wasn't there before.

"Daddy!" she shrieked, jumping in my arms. Her excitement and how tightly she was hugging me had any doubt I was feeling melt away. Just like my OG told me, I was the only father my baby girl had ever known and as far as I was concerned, it was going to stay that way.

"Hey baby—"

"I missed you, where you been? You missed my tooth coming out," she cut me off, pulling away just enough to point it out to me. As if I hadn't already noticed, I feigned a look of shock, inspecting it like I'd never seen a missing tooth before.

"Oh damn, you snaggle toothed again? How you gone eat chicken nuggets with a missing front tooth?" The question sent her into a fit of giggles.

"I can still eat. Mommy bought me McDonald's the day it fell out." She rolled her eyes like I was slow, and I couldn't help but laugh until I looked up to see Sha'ron standing in the doorway. Instantly, the smile on my face dropped. While my love for my baby had only intensified, any type of feelings I had for her mother had completely disappeared and it took everything in me not to fuck her up.

"Did you at least get some decent money from the tooth

fairy?" I quizzed, keeping my eyes on her mother, who was standing there with her face all balled up. My baby was talking a mile a minute about the five dollars she'd gotten and I was listening intently, not wanting to miss a single detail.

"Umm, Kay Kay, you need to go finish getting ready for school!"

My jaw tightened at Sha'ron's hating ass interrupting us but instead of blowing up like I wanted to, I dropped a quick kiss on my baby's cheek. "Go ahead, I'll drive you today and get you some Starbucks before I drop you off." That was more than enough to make her smile return. She took off running into the house, leaving me and her mama alone. I was fully prepared to ignore her and just wait for Kay Kay to get ready as I stepped inside, but that would've been too much like right.

"So you're not going to explain where you been and why the fuck you ain't been answering me and your daughter's calls for the last two days?" she started up as soon as the door shut behind me.

"I was sick."

I kept my answer short, hoping she'd carry her ass on somewhere, but again, that would've been too much like right.

"Siiiiick? Yo' ass wasn't never so sick you couldn't use your hands! Nah, you think you slick. Kay Kay already told me about you having her around some random! You so far up that bitch ass you ain't even talked to yo' mama in days either! No wonder you ain't tryna fuck me no mo—" Her words were instantly cut off by my hand wrapping tightly around her neck.

"See, that's yo' fuckin' problem. You don't know how to leave well enough alone!" I seethed, enjoying the fear that washed over her face way more than I should have. "A nigga really was sick after finding out yo' hoe ass been fuckin' Bronx and that Kay Kay might be his. You lucky I love that lil' girl to death, or else I'd leave you rotting right along with yo' nigga," I spoke lowly, wanting to push her dumb ass through the wall. My grip tightened around her throat as she flapped her lips and her eyes bugged out of her head.

"Yeah, and from now on, your best bet is to not say shit to me unless you're ready to die too." Hearing Kay Kay's feet thundering back down the stairs, I gave her a warning look and let her go. Immediately, she bent down, supporting herself against the wall as she gulped down air dramatically.

"You, ass...hole," she gasped, mugging me.

"I'm ready, Daddy!" My baby came around the corner and took us both in with a look of concern before going over to Sha'ron. "What's wrong with Mommy?" she questioned, and I was glad Sha'ron's ass could barely speak just in case she decided not to heed my warning.

"She choked on a peppermint. She'll be ayite. Let's go so we're not late grabbing your drink." Mentioning Starbucks was more than enough to snatch her attention. She quickly gave Sha'ron a kiss and told her she hoped she felt better before tucking her small hand in mine and pulling me to the door. I made sure to give her mama one last look, daring her to try me, before finally following Kay Kay out to my car. It was going to be in her best interest to do what I said, or else I'd make good on my threat and have her meeting Bronx in hell.

CHAPTER FIVE

HEAVY

After dropping my baby off with her peppermint hot chocolate, I stopped through my traps to do pickups since it hadn't been getting done. Doing the shit alone took a lot longer than usual and by the time I finished Kay Kay was about to get out of school. I'd promised to pick her little ass up and take her to dinner at my OG's restaurant, but I didn't play about having her around business shit. The type of shit I was into was risky as fuck and I did my best to keep her far removed from it. So having her in a car with a couple hundred thousand in drug money was out of the question.

Checking the time, I saw I only had about twenty minutes to be at her school, and even if I pushed it I'd still be a few minutes late. I raced home, parking my car in the garage, and jumped in my truck, watching the clock closely. The trip to my crib took me out my way and had me breaking every traffic law as I sped, cutting people off and running red lights.

When I finally swerved into the pickup area it was completely empty besides Kay Kay, her teacher, and her friend whose party we went to. Seeing another kid there despite the teacher's obvious frustration made me feel better about how late I was. I couldn't deny being surprised that Niko or his weird ass wife were late also though.

"You're late, Daddy," Kay Kay immediately went in on me with her little face balled up.

"My bad, snaggy," I told her, throwing my hands up defensively. I'd just gotten back in her good graces and the last thing I wanted was for her to be pissed off at me again. Backing up, I opened the door for her as I acknowledged her teacher and repeated my apology. "Sorry for being late, I got caught up with work. It won't happen again."

"It's okay, Mr. Stone, as you can see, you're not the only parent that sometimes runs late. At least it's not every day like some people," she said smartly, nodding in Kaliyah's direction before looking down at her watch. I could tell she had to be fed up with the situation to be speaking so candidly to a random ass person about another student's personal business.

"Right." Scratching the back of my neck in discomfort, I started to walk off.

"Daddy, can we take Kaliyah home? We already know where she lives," my baby rolled her window down and asked with her hands clasped together and puppy dog eyes.

"We can't do that, baby, we don't even know if somebody's at her house to get her—"

"Then can she come with us to go eat? It'll be somebody there by then. Pleeeeeeease!" I'd forgotten all about dinner, but her bringing it up instantly gave me an idea. Turning back to the teacher, I gave her my most charming smile.

"You know what, I actually can take her so you can head on out," I offered, noting the immediate doubt on her face. Legally she probably wasn't supposed to do what I was asking her to, and I knew damn well I'd blow her damn brains out if she did the shit with my kid. That didn't stop me from pulling out my phone to show her Black's contact. "Look, I know her parents personally. Well, her dad anyway, we do business together. I'll shoot him a text right now to let him know I got her."

Silently, she looked between me and the screen, weighing her options while both girls begged annoyingly. Finally, after a few seconds, she nodded with a heavy sigh. I was sure the fact that almost an hour had passed since school let out aided in her answer, but either way I was able to escort an excited Kaliyah into the backseat. I actually did send a text to Black's bitch ass before pulling off just so he'd know I had her when him and his wife finally realized they'd forgotten her. They spent the entire drive giggling and trying to play DJ from the backseat. Occasionally, I glanced in the rearview at her, unable to deny her resemblance to Adore. Baby girl had shorty's whole face and I wanted to kick Black's ass for keeping her away from her mama for so long. I always felt like that nigga was a bitch, but the way he was doing Adore only proved that shit even more.

"Ooooh, you gonna looooove my granny's food! She makes the best everything! And she'll make sure you get dessert!" Kay Kay gushed as we pulled in front of my mama's restaurant, and I couldn't do shit but laugh because she wasn't lying. If my baby divulged that Kaliyah's parents didn't give her many sweets she was probably going to give her ass as much dessert as she could eat, if her little stomach could even handle it after stuffing her with food.

Helping them out of the back, I let them run ahead while I ignored another call from Black. Suddenly, he was so concerned about his daughter even though he hadn't made sure somebody picked her up from school. I low key wanted to make him sweat, but instead, I went ahead and let him know we were grabbing a quick bite so the girls could hang out and that she was fine. Slipping my phone back in my pocket, I followed the girls inside, ignoring the way Felicia's funny looking ass was eyeballing me.

"Heeeey Heavy—"

"Is Adore here? Put us in her section," I cut her off, smirking inwardly when she sucked her teeth and snatched up some menus, answering my question. As usual the place was packed and I was glad there was even a spot left in Adore's section. I scanned the room and caught her coming out of the kitchen carrying a tray of drinks. As soon as she saw me she blushed and waved with her free hand, unable to see the kids over the sea of people. Even tired with her hair beginning to fall out of her messy bun, she was still gorgeous as fuck and I couldn't wait until she saw my little surprise.

Once we were seated, Felicia slapped the menus down and damn near stomped off. I made a mental note to check her about that shit later. One thing I didn't play about was somebody treating my baby funny 'cause they were mad at me. Flexing my fingers, I shook off my agitation, handing each of the girls their menus, and like a true expert, Kay Kay pointed out all the good things to eat.

They were both still browsing, hidden behind their menus, when Adore finally made her way around to us. "Oh, I didn't know you had company! Is that little Miss Kay Kay?" She grinned, pulling the menu down.

"Heeeey Adore! I brought my friend Ka—"

"*Ka-Kaliyah!*" Adore gasped, stumbling back a couple steps as her eyes watered. I grinned in satisfaction when she looked between the confused girls and me.

"You already met her?" Kay Kay's little nose crinkled and she tilted her head.

"No, I don't know her." Kaliyah's expression mirrored my baby's, and I lifted my brows at Adore, hoping she had a quick save since I hadn't thought that far ahead.

"Oh, I um... I know your parents, plus I've seen your picture in the paper with your granddad before. He's the mayor, right?" She finally got it together and the answer seemed to please Kaliyah, who rolled her eyes with a nod.

"Yeah, he is," she answered dryly, obviously just as annoyed by her granddaddy as she was with her parents. I could definitely understand that because I couldn't stand any of their asses.

"Well, it's nice to officially meet you, beautiful," Adore choked out, making Kaliyah blush.

"Thanks, it's nice to meet you too."

I peeped Adore discreetly wipe her face, before taking a deep breath. "What can I get you two gorgeous lil' ladies?" she asked once she gathered herself. Despite the amount of time they'd perused the menu, they still hadn't figured out what they wanted. After running down the list of specials, she got them both to decide on the catfish dinners with Sprite to drink. I ordered the soul food platter just to put something on my stomach because I hadn't eaten since the breakfast sandwich I had that morning.

Adore jotted down our orders then disappeared to grab the drinks, and my thirsty ass told the girls I'd be right back so I could follow her. I needed to see where her head was at because I knew me just popping up with her shorty had thrown her off. I caught her just as she grabbed some glasses.

"Heavy! When—how did you—" she quizzed frantically, catching herself before she said too much in the crowded kitchen. All eyes were already on us as usual, so I pulled her aside.

"She goes to the same school as Kaylani and whoever was supposed to pick her up was late, so I brought her with us." From where we were standing she had a perfect view of the girls, but when I said that her attention immediately turned back to me.

"What! That muthafucka forgot to pick up my baby!"

"I said they were late, calm down, mama bear. Plus, I don't even know if Niko's bitch ass was the one who was s'posed to pick her up anyway. Shit, the teacher said they always late."

"So, it was that bitch?"

"Maaan, chill. I done brought yo' baby to see you and yo' ass ready to send this bitch to the moon." Forgetting about our audience, I pulled her to me by her belt loops. "Look, fuck all that. Come eat with us and get to know Kaliyah. We can worry about all that other shit later." I could already tell her ass was about to start crying again, and I prepared to calm her down just as a commotion sounded in the front of the restaurant.

"Kaliyah! Kaliyah!" I immediately recognized Black's voice and knew shit was about to get ugly.

CHAPTER SIX

ADORE

I'd barely made out my baby daddy's voice when I saw him come storming up to the table where the girls were. I was so caught off guard that it took me a second to jump into action, even beating Heavy over, and his eyes ballooned when he saw me.

"I should've known you had something to do with this! Like, are you dumb or are you stupid, because surely you know this is considered kidnapping!" He immediately began berating me as he beckoned a crying Kaliyah from her seat.

"First of all, I work here, so I didn't have anything to do with shit! Maybe if you and yo' ignorant ass wife were doing your jobs, *our* daughter wouldn't be late getting picked up every day!" I didn't even realize what I said until multiple gasps and murmurs erupted around the room.

"You stupid, low life bitch!" he shouted, lunging forward, but Heavy moved in front of me and shoved him back a few feet.

"Nah, you stupid if you think I'm bouta let you touch her. I ain't gone say too much 'cause these kids around, but you know how ugly this shit can get, Black. Walk up outta here while you still can." Heavy's voice was low, but the threat was evident and Niko clearly felt it. A series of different emotions flashed across his face as he stood upright and straightened his suit.

"Wait until my father hears about this!" he fumed, looking from Heavy to me.

"You know damn well you the only one scared of yo' daddy." With a teasing grin, Heavy reached back for Kay Kay, who was still sitting down, too shocked to move. "Come say goodbye to your friend, baby." She eased out of her chair and moved toward Kaylani like her daddy told her to. It wasn't far to travel and they met around the side of the table, giving each other tight hugs as they both mumbled to each other. While Kay Kay seemed perfectly okay in the tense setting, Kaliyah was visibly upset and rightfully so. Not only had she witnessed her daddy acting a plum fool, but I was sure she'd caught on to what I said. I could only imagine what was going through her mind and before I could stop myself, I pulled her into a tight hug that she awkwardly returned.

"Kaliyah, let's go!" Niko huffed indignantly.

Her little face was conflicted, probably going through every memory she ever had to see if there was any truth to my words. "Are you really my mom?" she wanted to know, perfectly shaped brows bunching as she asked.

"Kaliyah!" I glanced around her to see smoke damn near coming out of Niko's ears. Swallowing hard, I put my attention back on my baby.

"I am... It's probably hard to believe and I know I need to explain how this is possible but—"

"Your eyes are the same color as mine," she noted, cutting

me off, and I realized she'd been studying my face the whole time. I couldn't help smiling as tears slipped out over my cheeks, and I nodded eagerly.

"Yeah, yeah I do, baby." My voice came out just barely above a whisper. It was hard to believe that I was actually having a conversation with my baby, and even harder to believe that we were having this type of conversation. I prepared myself to answer any other questions she may have, but she was quickly snatched away.

"I said let's go!" Niko grumbled as he held tightly to her arm.

"Don't touch her like that!" Standing, I took a couple steps toward them.

"Take your stupid ass back to work and let me worry about *my* child!" he tossed out over his shoulder as he made his way to the door, pausing slightly when he saw all the camera phones pointed his way. His discomfort at being scrutinized by a room full of people was obvious from the look on his face before he rushed out, trying to cover his face. The whole restaurant had tuned in to our drama and even though I should've been bothered, I was more focused on the fact that I'd finally met my daughter. Being so close to her only made me want to fight harder and get her away from the Black family for good.

———

"Oh my god! Do you think she believed you?" Isis asked with a spoonful of soup hovering over her bowl. It was the next day after the whole ordeal with Niko and being able to hold and talk to Kaliyah was all I could think about.

Shrugging, I took a sip of my strawberry tea. "I mean, I

think so. She even pointed out that we have the same eyes. I just wish we'd met under different circumstances. You should've seen the way Niko was acting, he only made shit that much worse." Out of every regret I had, I really wished I would've punched his ass in the mouth. He had been hurling a lot of insults and acting like he was so much better than me, when we both knew that if given the chance, he'd lick the jam from between my toes.

"Well, that definitely sounds like she believes you or is at least curious about what she's been told. That's a good start. As far as De'Niko though, fuck him and his prissy ass wife! Hell, fuck his mama and daddy too! All their asses can get it over my niece!"

"I swear that's the same thing Quay's crazy ass said. Let me find out y'all muhfuckas think alike." I laughed, but it quickly fell flat when I saw the way she tensed and put her attention on her food. "Oh naw, what the fuck done happened now? I thought y'all were good." Her reaction to my mention of Quay had my bestie senses tingling, and I hoped he hadn't done anything too stupid. Seeing them together, I could tell how much they loved each other even when she was in denial about their status. Still, it was only so much my girl was going to take.

"We were. I mean, I thought we were, but I guess not." She snorted with a roll of her eyes. "You remember the dude Bronx I was talking to? Well, apparently his grimy ass the one who shot Quay." My jaw dropped, but I quickly tried to recover as different thoughts ran through my mind. I hadn't talked to my brother much about his shooting, mainly because I didn't want to bring up such a traumatic experience. Maybe I should've though. Suddenly, my eyes widened as a thought came to me.

"Biiiitch! He probably used you to get to Quay! I know he

ain't mad at yo' ass about *that*?" Tossing her hands up, she rolled her eyes again.

"Exactly! You know how niggas is though. They already be feeling some type of way when it's another man involved, but it's even worse when it's one of their opps."

"True, but damn girl, you need a drink for the type of drama you got goin' on. Let's get mimosas!" I gushed, catching sight of our waitress and waving her over.

"I uh—I can't," she stuttered, lifting her drink with shifty eyes. That immediately alarmed me and I raised a suspicious brow as I waited on her to elaborate. "I'm...pregnant."

"Wait, I'm gone be an aunty? Bitch, tell me everything! How far along are you? When did you find out? Does Quay know already?" I bounced around in my seat, unable to contain my excitement while I waited for her to fill me in, even though she didn't look anywhere near as thrilled as me.

"It's funny you already know it's Quay's but his ass don't." She chuckled bitterly, shaking her head and instantly pissing me off. I just knew damn well Quay wasn't on the same shit as our bum ass daddy. He definitely hadn't sounded like anything was wrong with him the few times I'd seen his ass in the past couple weeks.

"Oh, I'm gone fuck him up! I know he not denying y'all's baby!"

"It's cool, boo. He wants a test and I'm gone give his ass one as soon as the doctor tells me I can so he can eat every word he spoke to me." Despite the hard front she was putting on, I could tell my friend was hurt behind my brother's actions and whatever he might have said. I changed the subject, getting her to talk about lighter things like her next appointment and due date. Poor thing seemed to have made up her mind about the test, but I spent the rest of our lunch date trying to convince her stubborn ass to wait until the baby was born. Even if she didn't agree though, I planned to get on Ja'Quay's ass until he did what he was supposed to do, especially if that counted stopping his baby mama from going through with such a risky surgery.

CHAPTER SEVEN

ISIS

I t had been weeks since I'd seen or spoken to Quay. As bad as it hurt, I'd long since realized he wasn't going to come around so easily. I wasn't going to stress about it though. I had an appointment to check on my baby and I didn't need my blood pressure going up thinking about its father. Just him popping up in my mind blew me and had me sucking my teeth as I tried to wiggle into my favorite jeans.

"Aww, hell naw!" I groaned, still pulling at my jeans even though I knew they wouldn't fit. "No, no, no!" I continued stuffing my thick thighs in but only managing to get it to my waist. Frustrated, I fell back on the bed to catch my breath. Apparently my pudge had gotten much bigger since even the day before, and suddenly none of my clothes fit. Not having reached this stage of pregnancy had me delusional because I definitely thought I had plenty of time before I would be needing new clothes.

Sighing, I went ahead and traded in my jeans for a baggy pair of maroon sweats and a black graphic tee. According to my doctor this was going to be a quick appointment, so there wasn't a need to get all cute anyway. Once I left I'd go shopping and pick up a few things for myself and a strawberry milkshake, which had been something I'd been thinking about all morning. I was brushing my thirty-inch, jet-black, middle-part bust down when my doorbell rang, and I immediately rolled my eyes, knowing it was probably Adore. She'd been pretty busy with Meka working on her article, but she'd insisted on coming with me to the appointment. I thought for sure with everything she had going on she'd be too tired to be dragged to an 8 A.M. appointment, but I guess I was wrong. I hurriedly finished brushing my bone-straight hair, unable to resist doing a quick, overexaggerated hair flip with my tongue out. I looked good as fuck and the extra pounds only added to how fine I was. They hadn't lied about the pregnancy glow. I was glad to be blessed with clear, glowing skin and I prayed it stayed that way for the rest of my pregnancy. The doorbell rang again, snatching me out of my thoughts. Sitting the brush down, I padded to the front to let my girl in. I already knew it was cold as hell out and that just reminded me I needed a coat too.

I opened the door without looking first. "Girl, I told you you didn't have to..." my voice trailed off at the sight of Quay and I fought hard not to immediately slam the door in his face. Despite being mad as hell at him and slightly scared, there was no denying the fluttering in my belly from seeing him after so long. I felt like a whole punk ass bitch for walking around looking a mess and pouring myself into work while he looked like he was thriving. Not at all like he'd been struggling with our discord. I noted his fresh haircut and shave, the bright diamond studs in his ears, and the blinged-out Cuban around his neck. Rocking a black and orange flannel, black straight-leg

Levi's, and construction Timbs, he looked and smelled down-right sexy. It took me a second to gather myself, but once I felt like I wasn't going to offer him some pussy as soon as I opened my mouth, I folded my arms and cocked my head up at him.

"Can I help you?"

He sneered at the question and easily moved me out of the way, brushing past with ease. "Why the key don't work?" He was still making his way through my apartment while I stood at the open door puzzled as fuck. The last time I'd seen him, he'd threatened to kill me and insisted that I stay away until I could prove our baby's paternity. I glanced at the clock on my wall and saw that I still had almost an hour before my appointment. If I wanted to make it on time I needed to be leaving soon, so I didn't have time to play with Quay's crazy ass. Rolling my eyes, I shut and locked the front door and headed back toward my bedroom.

"Aye, I know yo' ass heard me." He caught my arm as I passed him and I quickly snatched away. "You changed the fuckin' locks?"

"I don't have time for this bipolar shit, Ja'Quay! I have a doctor's appointment—"

"Why yo' ass think I'm here?" he cut me off with a sigh. At a loss for words, I opened and closed my mouth a few times before pursing my lips.

"I really don't know. It's too early to get the test done, but I'll let Adore know so she can tell you and we'll go from there." He glared down at me with dark eyes and I instinctively shrank away from him.

"Maaan, go finish getting ready," he ordered, giving me a light push toward my room as his phone rang. Right away I felt like he was trying to get rid of me so his ass could cake on the phone, and I couldn't help being a little jealous. He was already heading to the couch with the phone to his ear. As bad as I wanted to act a fool, I decided I wouldn't give his ass the satisfaction. While he talked I took my ass in my bedroom to finish getting ready. I slipped on my pink and maroon Air Maxes and sprayed myself with my Dior perfume.

By the time I grabbed my purse, phone, and keys and came back to the living room he was off the phone. He'd helped himself to some snacks and was sitting there crunching on a bag of Flamin' Hots, but he stood up as soon as he saw me.

"Ain't hot shit bad for the baby?"

"Not in moderation, now come on so I can lock up." I made sure to avoid looking directly at him as I beckoned his ass to the front door. Surprisingly, he didn't have a smart ass reply, but he didn't keep the same energy once we were outside.

"Where you goin'?" he questioned from behind me as I switched to my car.

"To the doctor—"

"What the fuck, man! Stop playin' with me and get yo' slow ass in this car, Ice!"

"No! I need to go shopping for clothes after this and I ain't tryin' to come all the way back here to get my car!" I snapped, matching the mug on his face with one of my own. His ass was really crazy to pop up on me demanding shit like nothing had happened. He was lucky that I was even willing to talk to him after what he'd done to me.

"Get in the car, Ice." This time his demand came much softer, but it wasn't any less threatening and I prepared myself to decline again, when Carmise came switching up the street.

"Heeeey, Quay," she gushed, batting her lashes and cheesing all hard before rolling her eyes at me. I was used to her being thirsty, but that didn't stop my nose from turning up in disgust at how disrespectful she was being. I watched as she put an extra sway in her hips and so did Quay, but once he saw me looking he ducked into his car. Just that fast, he no longer wanted me to get in the car with him, but that was cool with me because I didn't want to ride with his ass anyway.

He ended up beating me to the doctor's office and by the time I pulled up, he was leaning against his car waiting for me. Annoyed, I walked right past him to the building and held the door open for an expecting couple. They looked cute and I wondered if Quay and I would be that cordial soon. It clearly all depended on his crazy ass though.

Thankfully we made it through the appointment without any issues. We listened to the heartbeat and I let her know a few of my concerns, mainly about the rapid weight gain. Which she claimed was different for everyone. I caught Quay looking almost excited a few times but it didn't last long. His face would immediately turn stoic again whenever we locked eyes. I assumed it was thoughts of him not being the father creeping in, and after I cleaned the gel off my belly I went ahead and asked the question he'd been dying to know the answer to.

"Dr. Smith, I know it's too early, but when would I be able to get a DNA test done?" My irritation with Quay overshadowed the embarrassment I felt for even having to ask as her smile slipped and she looked between the two of us uneasily.

"Oh, well, since you're past nine weeks you can actually do one now. All we need is some blood from Mom and a mouth swab from... Dad," she hesitated. "Would you like to set that up?"

"Yes, as soon as possible please."

"Okay, I'll send a nurse in to take those samples shortly." She awkwardly said her goodbyes and exited the room, reminding me to make another appointment in four weeks. Just like she said, two nurses came in a few minutes later and got the samples she'd need. They let me know our results could take up to two weeks since the lab was backed up. Now I just needed to wait a couple of weeks and I'd be able to prove to Quay that this was his baby. I could hardly wait and once the truth came out, I was going to rub that shit in his face.

CHAPTER EIGHT

QUAY

I watched as my dick disappeared down Carmise's throat with ease, making my toes curl up in my boots. After the day I had, I needed the type of stress reliever that only someone's top could give and at the moment, Carmise was that someone. Really I had a few head doctors I could've called, but the biggest draw to her was her proximity to Isis. As dirty as she'd done me, it was only right I returned the favor. She was lucky her best friend happened to be related to me, that's how grimy I wanted to do her. Fucking my enemy was a line I never thought Ice would cross, and it had me questioning everything about her. I was at least relieved that we were able to do the test so I'd know if that was my baby sooner rather than later.

Before I knew it, I was spraying the back of shorty's throat with my kids and every bit of tension I'd been feeling left my body at the same time. She swallowed every drop too, looking up at me like a puppy as she pulled my dick from her mouth, simultaneously stroking and placing soft kisses on it. My shit was still semi-hard, but she quickly brought it completely back to life.

"You gon' finally give me some dick now?" she moaned, slowly stroking my dick like it was a prized possession.

"I'm straight," I told her dryly and got ready to stand, but her strong ass stopped me with a hand on my chest. Seeing she'd fucked up, she tried to smooth it over by sucking my balls into her mouth. Regardless of how fucked up it sounded, I'd prided myself on never actually sticking my dick in the women I messed around on Isis with. Besides sex being an extremely intimate act, I was firm on this being Ice's dick. Of course, she'd fucked that up, but a part of me still had to feel that way, which was why I hadn't fucked nobody else. I felt stupid for extending that level of loyalty to a bitch that clearly didn't even know what that word meant. That thought along with Carmise stroking my dick took the fight out of me.

When she saw me relax against the couch she produced a brand-new box of Magnums and handed them to me. Being a street nigga, I knew better than to accept a rubber from a jump off, but the fact that it was sealed and didn't look tampered with put me even more at ease. Opening the pack, I made sure to check the gold packaging before tearing it open and sliding it on. Shorty's eyes lit up and she gleefully stood, giving me a full view of her body in the pink cropped tank and black G-string she wore. She was acting like she'd waited for this moment her whole life, being all extra and swaying like it was some music playing. Little did she know, I wasn't interested in seeing her dance unless she was twerking on my dick.

"Maaaan, you tryna fuck or audition for *P-Valley*?" I asked irritably, making her slow ass giggle. Tossing her long ass weave over her shoulder, she wiggled out of her clothes, revealing a clean shaven pussy. Her shit was fat as hell and I had to get a closer look when I noticed the silver ring there. In all my years of fucking, I'd never met a woman with a piercing down there. With a smirk, she propped her leg up on the arm of the couch and spread her pussy lips apart so I could fully see it glistening from her juices.

"Mmmh, you see how wet it is?" She rubbed her clit until her fingers were saturated. "You wanna taste? Niggas say it's like biting into a juicy peach." Moaning, she thrusted in my face and I damn near caught whiplash from how fast I jumped back. The only only pussy I'd ever had in my mouth was Ice's and I planned to keep it that way. Even if I had been willing to, she'd blown me talking about "niggas." I was a grown ass man so I wasn't stupid enough to clock a woman's pussy, but in the heat of the moment no man wanted to hear about what other niggas said or did with a bitch he was currently fucking.

The look I gave said "stop playing with me," and she quickly got the message. Sucking her teeth, she braced herself with my shoulders and slowly eased down until I completely filled her up.

"Ssssss, shit!" she hissed, closing her eyes in ecstasy, and I had to admit I was feeling the same way. Despite how promiscuous she seemed, her pussy was virgin tight. She recovered from the initial feeling before I did, but I gripped her waist to keep her still. When I finally got my dick under control I tapped her side, giving her the green light. With low lids she took her time sliding up and down my pole. Her perky B-cups bounced in my face. I squeezed the left one while sucking her right nipple in my mouth before switching. The double stimulation had her getting loud as hell, and I didn't mind at first until she began screaming my name. "Yes, right there, baby! You fuckin' me so goooood, Quay!"

"Aye, shut the fuck up!" I tried to sound stern, but the chokehold she had on my dick made that shit come out weak as hell.

"I caaaaan't! Quay, baaaaby!" she whined, twisting her hips in a way that pulled me in deeper. It was obvious her ass was trying to put on a show. Switching up the pace, she planted her feet on each side of me and began bouncing. I took that moment to wrap my hand around her neck, squeezing just tight enough to shut her up. Her face twisted as she contracted around my dick, and her eyes rolled to the back of her head. She was still trying to recover when I grabbed up two handfuls of her ass and slammed into her repeatedly until I filled the condom with a grunt. Panting, I rested my head against her shoulder, ready for a fat blunt and my bed.

"Watch out." I tapped her leg and when she didn't immediately move, I lifted her off me, damn near tossing her onto the other cushion. Ignoring the pissed off look on her face, I climbed to my feet, removing the condom as I made my way to the bathroom to flush it.

When I came back she was still sitting on the couch with her robe on, pouting. I honestly didn't know what she thought that was going to do. Instead of paying her any attention, I grabbed my phone and keys.

"Wait, you leavin'?" Her eyes bugged in shock.

"Yeah, I got some shit to do," I said in a dry tone, unsure of why I was even as irritated as I was. Her following me around asking questions didn't help though.

"Are you comin' back? I can make you something to eat quick," she pressed, trailing me so closely she stepped on the back of my shoes.

"Back yo' ass up off me! I told you I had something to do! Fuck is you following me for!" I spun around on her fast and she instantly froze up, eyes big as saucers. I didn't really mean to blow up at her like that, but I wasn't in the mood to play twenty questions with her ass. She was lucky I'd even answered her to begin with. Her forehead bunched and she let out a bitter chuckle.

"Oh, you got the wrong bitch! Don't be tryna act funny now when you was just knee deep in my pussy five minutes ago, Quay!"

By now we were on the porch and I winced at how loud her stupid ass was being. The truth was, I may have thought I wanted to hurt Isis, but I knew I'd be fucked up if she caught my black ass. It was only midnight, but the surprisingly deserted block was dead silent so there was a big chance she'd hear this bitch screaming my name. Nervously, I stole a glance at Isis's crib in time to see her bedroom light come on. The last thing I wanted or needed was for her to hear Carmise arguing with me.

Not wanting to antagonize her crazy ass any more than she already was, I gave her my back and started down the stairs. Unfortunately, she'd already peeped me looking next door.

"Ohhhh, you don't want yo' bitch to know you over here, Quay! Fuck Isis boujie ass and fuck you too, Quay! You best believe I'm gone make sure she find out how many times you been over here fuckin' me and letting me sit on yo' face, Quay!"

"Bitch, you a fuckin' lie! You wish I would put my mouth on that rancid ass pussy!" I barked, spinning around on the last step, unable to let her dumb ass slide for that bullshit.

"Pussy couldn't be too rancid, you was just tearing this shit up like leftovers from thanksgiving, Quay!" My mama had raised me not to put my hands on women, but I was seconds away from choke slamming her in the middle of the street. It was best I got the fuck out of there before I could no longer control myself, but I was definitely going to pay some chicks to beat her ass.

"I ain't bouta argue with yo' desperate ass, bro," I scoffed, not wanting to give her any more attention.

"That's 'cause it ain't no point, Quay! You can't deny it anyway when you walkin' around smellin' like you just bathed in my pussy juice, Quay!" The sound of a door slamming shut drew my attention back to Isis's house. The light in her front room was now on, but suddenly shut off, letting me know that it was definitely her door I'd heard. Like the thirsty bitch she was, Carmise cackled as she followed my gaze next door. Pissed, I couldn't even do shit but curse while Carmise strutted her messy ass inside.

"Bye, Quay!"

I was still irritated the next day and the shit had me snapping at everybody in my crew. It seemed like everything they did pissed me off, and at the point that I almost came to blows with one of the corner boys over five dollars, Manny told me he'd handle it and sent my ass home. I was hungry though, so I took a detour to my mama's crib, knowing that she or Adore had cooked something.

As soon as I stepped inside I wasn't disappointed as the smell of fried chicken filled my nostrils. "Aye Ma! Adore!" I shouted from the doorway, only to be met with silence. It was probably the loud ass Anita Baker that was playing. Kicking off my Jordan's, I followed the music to the kitchen where I found my mama and sister drinking wine as they each stirred something on the stove. "It smell good as fuck in here! Let me get a plate with everything," I said, lowering the volume on their speaker.

"God dammit, Ja'Quay! Don't be sneaking up on me like that!" My mama's scary ass whipped around, clutching her chest dramatically while Adore mugged me. I could already tell her friend had been in her ear.

"Don't be lookin' at me like you tryna fight. And maybe if y'all asses wasn't in here blasting that old ass baby making music you would've heard me come in," I huffed, looking between the two of them as I plopped into a chair.

"It sound like somebody talkin'. Ma, do you hear somebody talkin'?" Adore's childish ass rolled her eyes and turned back to whatever she was stirring.

"You sound like a little ass kid, bro."

"No, *you're* the one sounding like a kid! You gotta whole baby on the way with the woman you supposed to love, but you're treating her like shit and acting like it's somebody else's baby."

"Aye, you don't know what the fuck you talkin' 'bout! I bet her black ass ain't tell you she was fuckin' my opp while she over there spilling her guts to you!" I was already in a bad mood, but knowing that Isis was going around running her mouth to my sister about our business had me livid. My mama hadn't even been made aware of anything that was going on and I'd planned to keep it that way at least until we got the DNA test back. I could already feel her eyes burning a hole in the side of my face.

"Actually, she did, but it's not like he walked up to her and said hey, I shot yo' nigga, let's fuck! If anything, he probably targeted her because of yo' ass!" she accused, pointing her bright ass nail at me, and my jaw clenched. I'd already considered that and no doubt it had me a little tight about the danger she could've been in because of me, but the only danger her ass ended up being in was being reckless with her pussy. *My pussy!*

"None of that shit matters. She lucky I'm even still talkin' to her ass considering I don't know whose baby that is!" Her eyes narrowed into slits and she walked off grumbling under her breath while my mama looked on silently.

"Ma—" I started, ready to plead my case, but she held up her hand to stop me.

"I'm not bouta let you kill my buzz with yo' early twenties drama, but let me just say if you left that girl and denied her baby off a hunch, then you ain't no better than Mike's bum ass."

"But Ma—"

"Didn't I just say I ain't tryna hear it! You and yo' sister just said an earful so an explanation is not needed. If you think that's not yo' baby and you wanna wait for a DNA test that's your right, but don't be crying about the time you missed out on being a stubborn fool. You know better than anybody what it's like not to have a father, and I just thought I'd raised you better than that is all I'm saying." Shrugging, she finished off her glass before moving back over to the stove. "Now this food almost done, so if you want a plate it'll be a few minutes."

"Nah, I'm straight," I huffed, even more irritated than I'd been when I got there. Unfazed, she kept cooking as I got up from the table and left. Bronx's dead ass had fucked up all types of shit with his revelation, and I wished I could kill him all over again. Pissed off and hungry, I stopped through a McDonald's that didn't smell nowhere near as good as my OG's food before taking my ass home where I didn't have to hear nobody's mouth.

CHAPTER NINE

HEAVY

With double the work since smoking Bronx, I had even less free time than before, but I'd figured out a remedy for that. I'd been trying to find a replacement for him but that shit was harder than I thought it would be. Having a nigga I'd been tight with since high school flipping on me had my level of trust fucked up. If my day one could have malice in his heart for me, then I needed to be selective as fuck the next time around. Every nigga on my team had been under intense scrutiny, but I didn't even feel like I could trust my own instincts at this point. That was why I was about to switch shit up.

"What up, big homie?" Quay announced himself and reached out for a pound before plopping down into the booth across from me. "Why yo' ass always tryna meet up in a restaurant like we Italians or some shit?"

"Shiiit, I love food and half the time, I be too busy running around to eat so I be tryna kill two birds with one stone." Shrugging, I pushed my menu toward him. "You want something?"

"Only to find out why the hell I had to meet yo' ass up here at the crack of dawn." He sighed, running a hand down his face, and I finally noticed how rough he looked. From what I knew of Quay he was always dressed to impress and alert, so I could only assume that he was dealing with some serious shit. Resting my arms on the table, I leaned in to ask.

"You straight?"

Sneering, he drew his head back. "That's what you had me come up here for? Did Adore say something to you?" he accused, squinting at me suspiciously, and I had to laugh.

"Nah, Adore ain't said shit about any issues between y'all, but if you got something on yo' mind I'm all ears." I shrugged. Even though a heart to heart wasn't a part of my plans, I didn't mind giving him some advice if he needed it. He swiped his nose and looked around like somebody might've been listening in.

"How you let the shit that nigga Bronx said just slide? Like, how you cool knowing it's a chance that ain't yo' shorty?" he quizzed, and I realized Bronx's last bitch move was the reason he was looking so stressed. Even after he had spazzed out the way he did that night, I was still hoping he would take my advice and not let the ramblings of a dead nigga fuck up his life. Clearly, that shit had gone over his head.

The waiter chose that moment to pop up so I quickly put our conversation on pause so I could order. I kept it simple and got the breakfast special, offering once again for Quay to get something, and as an afterthought he ordered the same. When the waiter walked off I went ahead and resumed the conversation.

"I can't lie, it had my head fucked up for a couple days. Shit had me sittin' up lookin' at pictures of my Kay Kay for hours tryna see if she had any of that nigga's features that I'd somehow overlooked." I scoffed, hating to say that shit out loud. "I got fucked up off some D'ussé and ignored my baby mama and my baby's calls. Shit, I was feelin' like a goofy! My OG stopped through on the second day and cursed my ass out. She gave me some shit to think about, and I realized whether we share the same DNA or not, I'm her daddy. Fuck Bronx."

I could damn near see the wheels turning as he considered what I said. Just seeing the type of grief he was still having over that shit had me feeling bad. Hell, I already felt bad about the little bit I'd seen the night we killed that nigga, and if he was still going through it then I could only imagine what else he'd done to his girl. Judging from the fucked-up look on his face, he'd been too pissed off to take time and consider the possibility of Bronx being a liar.

"My situation different though. I caught my girl at that nigga crib and shit, as far as the baby, I don't even know that lil' nigga yet! I mean, we got a test and shit so I'll know if it's mine sooner than I thought, but it's still the fact of her even fuckin' that nigga. One minute I'm cool and I think I can handle that shit, but every time I get around her dumb ass I remember she fucked my opp." He frowned as the waiter returned and set our plates down before disappearing again.

"I—"

"I probably took shit kinda far the night I found out. Upping my gun on her and saying I'd kill her ass was fucked up, but she's lucky I love her dumb ass too much to follow through with that shit. Now I done fucked her neighbor and she got the nerve to be mad at me like she might not be carrying the next nigga baby." My eyebrows shot up to my hairline at the revelation, and my ass had no idea what to say. I hadn't expected shit to get that deep. To be honest, I barely expected him to tell me shit, but he obviously felt like I could give him advice on what he had going on.

"Damn." I scratched the back of my neck uncomfortably,

not knowing where to start. "I can't lie, that's a lot for any woman to just forgive and forget, bro. Since y'all already took the test though, I'd wait until the results come back before making a move. That way you won't risk fucking up worse. If it comes back yo' baby then you gone have to put in extra work to get back on shorty good side, and if it's not yo' baby then you got a decision to make. You said you love her? Do you love her ass enough to look past her having a kid with somebody else?" I shrugged after posing the question, because it was really that simple to me. Then again, like he said, our situations were different. I couldn't say what I would've done if I found out Kay Kay wasn't my kid back when Sha'ron was pregnant. Thankfully, I didn't have to though. That shit was much easier to consider eight years down the line. Quay, on the other hand, was dealing with a real dilemma. I just hoped he hadn't taken shit too far that he couldn't get it back once he realized he wanted it back.

He grew silent once again, mulling over my advice before nodding and finally lifting his fork. "I feel you, big homie. I'ma chill and wait till these results come back and depending on what the muhfuckas say, I might need to chill and wait some more, but I ain't gone do no more crazy shit....for now."

"That's what's up." I didn't know if he'd be able to stick to that shit, but I felt like a proud big brother. Since that was straightened out, I finally started eating my food, completely forgetting about the original reason for the meeting.

"Oh shit, what you wanted to meet about again?" He tilted his head quizzically, clearly having forgotten too. I was glad he reminded me though, because him coming onboard with me would help occupy his time. Suddenly feeling like the previous conversation had led straight to this, I smirked.

"I think I might have a business proposition for you," I told him, and he hiked a questioning brow as I went into more detail. By the time the meal was over, I had myself a new right hand.

———————

"Daddy, are you goin' to the hotel to see Adore tonight?" Kay Kay questioned from the backseat, and I did a double take in the rearview. I was headed to drop her off to my OG so I could finally take Adore on the date I'd promised her. With all the shit I had going on I hadn't found the time, but after moving some things around I was able to plan something for her. Of course, the date landed on my weekend with my baby, but I figured a couple hours with her grandma wouldn't hurt. Apparently it did though, because I was confused as fuck about her line of questioning.

"Where you get that from, Kay Kay?" I tried to keep the alarm out of my voice as I looked between her and the road. She'd been playing on her iPad, but my tone had her little head popping up.

"Mama told her friends you take Adore to the hotel all the time." She shrugged like it was no big deal, and I clenched my teeth angrily. Since I'd checked her ass she'd been real quiet whenever I came around, but obviously she was still saying little slick shit around and to my baby.

"Nah baby, I'm taking her out to dinner. I don't take Adore to hotels." I chuckled uncomfortably, not knowing what I was supposed to say to some shit like that. No doubt her mama was going to get an earful from me as soon as I had a free minute to call her ass.

"I was bouta say, 'cause who goes to a hotel to have fun? I mean, the pool is fun but other than that, the only other thing to do is sleep and don't nobody wanna sleep." She balled her little face up and I breathed a sigh of relief that Sha'ron's stupid ass didn't go into details around her. Having baby mama drama was some shit I wasn't used to, because despite us breaking up, she was always cool. I was starting to realize she'd only been cool as long as I was giving her dick and not fucking with nobody else. Her antics were beginning to show me exactly how stupid she could get, and I had a feeling it was only going to get worse if I didn't get a handle on her.

CHAPTER TEN

ADORE

I stared at myself in the mirror as Isis wand curled my hair and could hardly believe how good I looked. Heavy was taking me on a date finally and I couldn't wait until he saw me. It was my first time actually dressing up, and even though my hair wasn't finished I felt like a whole model. I couldn't lie, my week had been going great and it had me in a good ass mood. They'd finally taken me off house arrest, Meka had finished the story and was waiting for her boss to review it, and now I was topping it off with a date with Heavy. A bitch was on cloud nine and I couldn't stop myself from smiling at my reflection.

"Look at you over here smiling to yourself like you in a romcom." Isis met my eyes in the mirror with a smirk. "That's that Heavy effect, huh?"

"I mean, he is kinda perfect, right?" I gushed, feeling a swarm of butterflies just from talking about him. Although things with Heavy were pretty new, he'd already shown me more care and kindness than any nigga I'd ever encountered. It was obvious that he wasn't only trying to get something from me, and I appreciated that more than anything.

"Fasho boo, and y'all better name y'all first baby after me too. Isis Jr. sounds good, don't you think? It just rolls off the tongue, right?" She stopped twisting my hair on the curlers long enough to look off dramatically.

"Oh, you trippin' now. Ain't nobody said nothin' about a baby. I'm good with Kaliyah, Kay Kay, and baby Quay here!" My voice came out high pitched as I turned enough to rub her small belly, but she immediately slapped my hand away.

"Aht, aht, don't do that. Don't be bringing that negative energy up in here." Rolling her eyes, she stuffed a strawberry licorice in her mouth and combed out another section of hair to curl. I didn't mean to put her wishy washy ass in a bad mood by bringing up my brother, but it was hard not to considering. I wasn't the type of sister that co-signed her brother's bullshit just because we were related, which was why I went so hard on him the last time I'd seen his ass. He was dead ass wrong for the way he was acting and I had no problem telling him so. I knew that hustling could make niggas paranoid and with good reason, because anybody could stab you in the back for the right price. However, I also knew that Isis wasn't like that. Despite his hoeish ways, Ja'Quay had done a lot for her and she loved his dirty draws too much to intentionally hurt him. I knew once his actual anger subsided he'd realize that he jumped the gun.

"Did he go to your appointment at least?" I asked, hoping that he had taken his stubborn ass over there like I told him to. He could have his feelings, but there was a baby involved and having the father around from day one was important, especially since this was a new experience for Isis. Her nose scrunched up at the question and she grumbled before biting into another piece of candy.

"He did, but he was acting like an asshole the whole time so I just asked Dr. Smith when was the soonest we could get a test done—"

"Isis!" I squealed, turning around, making her roll her eyes again.

"Calm down, girl. She said they can do it by drawing blood so the baby will be fine. Now turn around, 'cause yo' ass almost just got burned." My body instantly relaxed learning there wasn't any risk to the baby.

"Oh, okay."

"I had her do it right then and there so he can at least know the baby is his and I won't have to keep putting up with his bullshit. Now if only there was an over-the-counter lie detector test so I can also prove I didn't know who the hell Bronx was to him. He's been showing his ass and don't even know it's for nothin'." Whatever else she grumbled came out too low for me to catch, but before I could ask the doorbell rang. Our eyes met in the mirror and she smiled, mouthing, *he's here!*

"Adore! Dominique's here! Don't keep him waiting long, lil' girl!" We both laughed at my mama's antics as she finished up the last curl.

"Ok, all done. You've been beautified! Now hurry up and get down there to yo' man. You know we don't want yo' mama comin' up here to get yo' ass!" Isis cracked, turning the curlers off and setting them on my desk so they could cool off.

"I swear to god! Ain't no telling what she down there doing to him anyway." I took a second to primp in the mirror, pleased with the overall look, while Isis looked on like a proud mama. As happy as I was though, I felt bad for leaving right in the middle of our conversation. I waited while she quickly gathered her things so we could walk down together, and just before we reached the stairs I let her know.

"I really do hope he gets it together, best friend. I love y'all for each other and I don't want y'all into it for the rest of our lives over a misunderstanding."

"Girl, don't worry about that right now. We'll figure our shit out eventually, but until then I'm just gonna live vicariously through you and *Dominique*," she drawled with a chuckle. "Now come on, 'cause your niece or nephew hungry." Putting her free arm through mine, she helped me down the stairs where Heavy was sitting on the couch eating a piece of the Seven-Up cake my mama had baked while she sat across from him with heart eyes.

"Ma, why would you give him cake knowing we're going to dinner?" I asked, causing their eyes to shoot to me. While my mama looked completely unbothered and waved me off, Heavy instantly grinned like the cat that ate the canary. He took in my attire from the gold open-toed heels on my feet, to the purple chiffon dress that dipped low between my breasts and flowed to a stop just above my knees, finally landing on my beat face. Setting his plate on the coffee table, he stood to his feet.

"You look...amazing," he complimented, quickly closing the distance between us so that he could slip his arm around my waist. Just like every other time I was around him, my stomach was doing flips and my cheeks grew warm.

"Thanks, you do too." It was true. The black fitted turtleneck he wore fit him like a glove and so did the black slacks he'd paired them with. It was a completely different look for him and even though I liked the dressed down Heavy, it was something about him being dressed professionally that had me weak in the knees, and he smelled downright delicious.

"Compliments to the chef, 'cause he lookin' like he about to devour yo' ass," Isis tried to whisper in my ear, but the smirk on Heavy's face told me he had heard her loud and clear. She was lucky her ass was pregnant so I couldn't in good conscience elbow her mannish self like I wanted to.

"You do look absolutely beautiful, baby. Let me get a picture of y'all?" My mama was already pulling out her phone and motioning for us to get closer, if that was even possible.

"Oh my god, Ma, this ain't the prom." Despite my complaining, Heavy was already pulling me closer and looking at my mama with all thirty-two showing.

"So, you better pretend like it is and smile!"

I sucked my teeth but did as she said, and followed Heavy's lead as he went from the traditional poses to the prison ones that everybody made fun of. Isis even joined in for a few. She finally let us leave after Isis's stomach growled loud as hell. Feeding her grandbaby had become one of her favorite things to do, and since Isis was always hungry it worked out great.

"Man, I can't stop staring at yo' fine ass." Heavy sighed after we'd been driving for a while. "You laughing, but I don't know if I wanna share you tonight." He lifted my hand that was already enclosed in his to give it a light kiss.

"Damn, don't be stingy. Isis hooked me up too good for only one person to see it, even if it's you." Puckering my lips, I tossed my hair over my shoulder like a diva.

"I can't argue with the truth, muhfuckas just bet not look too hard."

His jealousy was cute, but I still sent up a little prayer that nobody tried him while we were out. I'd only ever seen a slightly irritated Heavy, I'd hate to see him mad enough to throw hands. Shuddering at the thought, I was brought back to reality when he gave my hand a light squeeze and pointed out a building on my side of the car. "This is it."

My eyebrows drew in at the sight of the warehouse-styled building. It looked abandoned and although there wasn't any broken windows or graffiti, I wasn't trying to go in there. Whipping my head around, I pointed as he pulled up.

"*This* is where we're going?" I asked, hoping his ass was lost or something, but he just chuckled and continued texting away on his phone.

"Yeah, it's cool though. I know you gone like this spot."

Now I was really looking at his ass crazy because I didn't know why he would think I'd like an abandoned building. "I'm not into that paranormal hunting shit if that's what you're thin—"

"Chill, you're in good hands, baby." He grinned before climbing out and coming around to open my door. Not moving, I just looked from his hand to his face with a raised brow, until he finally leaned in and unlatched my seatbelt for me. "Come on now, Adore. You know I wouldn't do anything to put you in harm's way. You're safe with me, mind, body, and soul." He looked deep into my eyes and I don't know how, but I believed him, relaxing enough for him to help me out of the car.

"Ahhh!" I clutched my chest when a random man came into view behind him. Alarm immediately clouded his features and he backed away.

"My bad, man," Heavy's ass laughed, handing him the keys and a hundred-dollar bill before turning to me. "He's the valet, crazy ass girl." He pulled my body against his side and I finally took notice of the man's uniform. He was dressed in the typical vest and bow tie that valets wore, but I still side eyed him as he gave a small wave and disappeared behind the wheel of Heavy's car, pulling off.

"It's not funny, Dominique, his ass came outta nowhere looking like he was about to throw us in a white van!" I huffed irritably, elbowing his side. He seemed completely unfazed and probably hadn't even felt it since his abs were so tight.

"I told you to trust me. Besides, he was too little to throw me anywhere!" he joked, leading me toward the entrance to the building that looked just as uninviting as the rest of the building. I already had a plan to kick my heels off and run out of there as soon as I saw something crazy, but my mouth damn near hit the floor once we stepped inside.

CHAPTER ELEVEN
ADORE

My feet were glued to the ground as Heavy held the door open for me and I stared inside in awe. The hallway was lined in red, from the walls to the carpet, and dimly lit with beautiful chandeliers that seemed to never end, giving it a romantic glow. An older black man stood off to the side dressed in a sharp suit and tie with a crisp white cloth draped over his forearm. I couldn't hide the shock on my face as I turned to Heavy, who winked at me and grinned cockily.

"Welcome to The Red Velvet Tavern. I'm Charles, the maître d'," the man drawled once we finally stepped inside. "Right this way." I tried to keep my composure, but on the inside I was ecstatic and trying hard not to squeal childishly. The further we followed Charles down the hall the more curious I became as the sound of quiet classical music grew louder. At the end of the long hall, he lifted the dark red curtain to show a dining room with white clothed tables with a long wooden bar against the right wall. Each table had water candles in the center that gave just enough light for the diners to see each other and shut everyone else out. It was surprisingly crowded considering how empty the street was.

Charles led us inside and over to a table of our own before snapping his fingers, and a waitress appeared out of nowhere with our menus and a water pitcher. She went to work quickly filling our glasses, and I looked over the menu while Heavy ordered some wine I couldn't pronounce. Once she had his request she disappeared just as fast as Charles had, leaving us alone.

"How'd you find out about this place? It's...*really* nice!" I lowered my menu and told him in a hushed tone. It was like some secret society restaurant and I was already blown away just from the ambiance alone.

"I got my ways." He shrugged, grinning when I narrowed my eyes at him. "Ayite, ayite. I know the owner. We did some business together in the past," he admitted just as the waitress returned with a dark bottle and poured us each a glass.

"Are you ready to order yet or do you need more time?"

Heavy immediately looked my way, but I still hadn't found anything I wanted. "Give us a few minutes, please," he told her with his eyes still on me. "Let's make a toast."

"A toast?" I raised a brow and picked up my glass. "What exactly are we toasting?"

"To our beginning," he said smoothly, licking his lips. I didn't know if it was the lack of sex in my life or just how fine he was, but I instantly ruined the dainty piece of fabric I was wearing as a thong.

Clenching my thighs together, I tapped my glass against his. "To our beginning."

A few days later I was all smiles as I prepared to get ready to meet Meka at her office. My date with Heavy had gone better than I could've expected. As always, he was a perfect gentleman, which I was quickly finding out only made me want him more. While he'd been trying to make sure I got home at a decent time, I was trying to figure out how I could trip and fall and land on his dick without looking like a hoe. The little bit of men I'd been around had always been thirsty to fuck and would do or say anything for some pussy, Niko included. Heavy was being patient and playing it cool though. *Fine ass!*

I was already dressed in a white, long-sleeve bodysuit with dark blue jeans and black leather thigh-high boots. My hair was in a half-up, half-down style that draped my shoulders. Fresh faced and wearing only lipgloss, I finished checking myself out and smiled at my reflection. Just that fast, my thoughts had gone from Heavy to my baby, and my meeting with Meka's boss was going to put me one step closer to her. I'd been both surprised and grateful when Heavy brought her to the restaurant. The way things were going, I thought I'd never get to see her in the flesh, but being able to had lit a fire in me. That and the way Niko had shown his ass. Although I hadn't wanted her to find out about me like that, I was glad she finally knew and wasn't immediately afraid of me. She had actually handled herself well for such a young girl, but her ninth birthday was coming up and I planned to be able to attend her party or at least throw her one of my own.

My phone dinged, notifying me that my Uber was almost there, so I grabbed my purse and headed downstairs. My mama was sitting on the couch watching TV in her favorite pink robe, but she immediately smiled when I entered the room. It was her off day so I hadn't wanted to bother her for a ride since she didn't get them often. "You goin' out with Heavy again?" she questioned with her thirsty self, and I couldn't help but laugh. He'd made a big impression on her. I could tell she liked him a lot because ever since our date she'd been asking about his ass.

"No Ma, I got that meeting with Meka and her boss." I shook my head at how pressed she was, but I was glad that she liked him.

"Oh, I forgot that was today. Do you need a ride?" she asked, already getting out of her comfy position to stand, but I waved her back down.

"Naw Ma, you enjoy your day off. I already ordered an Uber."

"Girl, we gone have to teach you how to drive. You gone mess around and give all your money to them people." She wasn't lying. In an effort to stay off public transportation I had started using Uber a lot, but it was going to have to do because I wasn't ready to get behind the wheel.

"Soon Ma, I ain't in no rush to drive in this mess though," I told her truthfully, and she nodded.

"They definitely drive like they ain't got no sense. Anyway, I think I found another lawyer to look at your case." I was quiet for a minute. I didn't want to disappoint her but I was honestly tired of getting my hopes up only for the lawyer to see the Black name and get scared. At this point it was a waste of gas and money just to go to their offices and be turned right around. Instead of telling her that though, I put on a forced smile.

"Great! We'll talk about it when I get back," I said, rushing out of the door. I was glad my Uber had pulled up because it was beginning to get too cold to just be standing outside. My driver, Latisha, was cool and we spent the entire ride making small talk. When I finally got to the building Meka worked in I blended right in with the sea of people bustling by. I got off on the fourth floor and the receptionist directed me through a maze of cubicles until I came to her door, knocking lightly before stepping inside.

"Hey Meka, I know I'm a little early but..." My words trailed off as I came face to face with Niko's mother. She looked the exact same with minimal signs of aging. Her face was made up in a soft beat and her hair was pulled into a perfect French roll. She was dressed in a black pantsuit that I knew cost thousands of dollars, matched with an equally expensive pair of Louboutin's. Her icy eyes landed on me, and I shrank under her scrutiny. Meka sat at her desk looking apologetic but not daring to speak as the woman I assumed was her boss stood nearby.

"Adore, still causing trouble, I see." She looked me over with her nose turned up, just like the last time we'd been in the same room together, except this time I wasn't afraid to speak my mind.

"About the same amount as your predator son and crooked husband." I shrugged, folding my arms as I enjoyed the shock that crossed her face. She wasn't used to me saying much of anything, but I was far from the scared seventeen-year-old she'd met the night I was arrested. Gathering herself, she smirked sinisterly.

"Umph, I heard that prison hardens people and you've obviously allowed your time inside to make you bold, but it didn't make you any smarter. You should know by now what my family is capable of. We've got our claws in this city from the police to parole officers, lawyers, judges, even journalists." She motioned around the room before pointing her finger at me. "This is the last and final warning you will get to leave our family alone. If not, I can make your life even more hell than it already is and trust me, you won't be able to recover." She had an accomplished look on her face like she'd really done something and was daring me to try her. Unfortunately for her, she'd finally broken me down to the point that I no longer cared about the consequences of my actions. I'd already lost eight years of my life, missed out on the opportunity to be there for my baby, and had my heart broken in the worst way. So when my feet started moving toward her, I was fully prepared to do the time for beating her ass the way I was about to, but Meka was faster. I didn't know if she hopped over her desk or flew over it, but she was standing between us before I could get within arm's length of the old bitch.

"Adore, don't! This is exactly what she wants you to do. Think about Kaliyah," she pleaded lowly so only I could hear as she pushed me back toward the door.

"Estelle, are you alright?" Her boss immediately went to check on her like she wasn't the biggest threat in the room, and I scoffed. I wasn't even surprised when Estelle smirked at me discreetly before playing it up like she was terrified. Her acting was terrible, but that didn't stop the woman from feeding right into it, ushering her over to a chair.

"You're a phony old bitch and I swear, you, your husband, and your son are going to get what's coming to you!" I was able to get out before Meka fully pushed me out of the room. I could already see security headed our way, and I wondered who had the time to call them.

"It's ok guys, I got her," Meka let them know, rushing me over to the elevators.

"What the fuck, Meka! What just happened back there? I thought we were meeting with your boss!" I seethed, turning my rage on her as angry tears burned my eyes.

"I-I don't know. Karla came busting into my office with her this morning and told me there was no way we could print the story. I tried to explain to her that you were already on your way here and Mrs. Black insisted she stay." She sighed, massaging her temple. "This shit is fucked up, Adore. I really wasn't expecting this to happen for real." I was too pissed off to speak so I just paced the small area and tried not to blow up. The truth was I should've been expecting something like this. The Blacks were able to shut down every attempt I made to out them and it was becoming obvious that just like Estelle said, they had ties to everyone. Today had just been another reminder of that fact. I was over trying to do things the right way. At this point, I was ready to fight fire with fire, fuck the contract.

Meka was still mumbling about how messed up it was as the elevator dinged. "It's okay, I know what I need to do. Thanks for trying though, Meka."

She looked at me curiously, confused by how calm I was all of a sudden, but I was already slipping into the elevator along with a few other people who were trying to leave the floor. I rode down to the lobby, hoping that what I was about to do wouldn't get my ass locked back up before I could see my baby again. Exiting the building, I immediately pulled my phone out and hopped on TikTok, which seemed to be the best way to spread news lately. Outing them on my own was clearly the only way, and hopefully if I got enough views I'd have more people willing to help me.

CHAPTER TWELVE
NIKO JR

"Mr. Black, your wife's on line one! She says it's an emergency!" my receptionist said after knocking and realizing it was locked. Rolling my eyes, I tried not to let the intrusion throw me off.

"Tell her I'll call her back!" I shouted and immediately bit my lip so as not to moan loudly as my mentee, Natasha, squeezed her pelvic muscles and threw her ass back. Attempting to gain some kind of control, I gripped her waist tightly, but that didn't slow her down at all.

"But—"

"Get the fuck away from my door and don't bother me again until I finish my session!" Instead of responding, I heard her heels clicking away, and I put my focus back on Natasha's ass as it rippled with each thrust.

"Mmm it's so sexy to see you take charge like that, daddy." She looked at me over her shoulder with a sexy pout, and my balls instantly began to tingle. As if she could see my nut coming, she went into overdrive, picking up speed as she slammed against me. The only sound that could be heard in the room was our skin slapping and me sliding through her wetness.

"Ohh, I'm about to fucking explode!"

"Hold on, baaaaby! I'm almost there," Natasha whined. Unfortunately, it was too late. Squeezing my eyes shut, I pushed myself as deep as I could and released. She tried to desperately keep grinding against my softening dick, hoping to get hers, but she clearly wasn't quick enough. I already knew what was coming next but still winced when she pushed me off her and looked at me with irritation. It was the exact same look that I'd gotten from almost every woman I slept with lately. At thirty-one, I was too young to have erectile problems, and according to my doctor I didn't have any, but that didn't stop me from having to use enhancements just to last longer than five minutes.

"Really nigga!" she snapped with her hands on her hips.

"Babe, I'm sorry I—"

"I don't wanna hear that weak ass shit! You're always sorry, Niko, and I always get left unsatisfied! Are you still fuckin' your wife?" With narrowed eyes, she shifted her weight from one foot to the other. Knowing how crazy she could be, I immediately shook my head emphatically.

"What, of course not! I told you I'm done with her, I'm only staying because of Kaliyah." My lies did nothing to stop the suspicious look she was giving me and I hoped my nerves weren't showing. "Let me just eat it for you before you go. You can sit on it," I said lowly, stepping closer to her and licking my lips. If I wasn't skilled at anything else, I could certainly bring a woman to orgasm with my tongue. Her lips curved into a smile and I knew I had her, but just as she melted into my embrace, the knob on my door was twisted furiously before someone began pounding on it.

"De'Niko! Why is this door locked? Let me in right this

instant!" The sound of my wife's voice quickly changed my irritation to fear as I locked eyes with Natasha. Pushing her away, I pulled my pants and underwear up, not bothering to remove the condom while she stood by watching.

"Sorry honey, just give me a second to—"

"Open this fucking door, Niko!" she shouted, hitting the door so hard I thought for sure it would come right off the hinges.

"*Fuck!* You need to get in the closet!" I struggled to straighten my clothes. Once I finished, I attempted to pick up the things on my desk that we'd knocked over, only to find Natasha still standing there with her face twisted in horror. "What the fuck are you doing?" I hissed, frantically snatching her up by the arm.

"Let me go! I ain't gettin' in no closet, fuck yo' wife! I don't care about that uptight bitch!" I didn't know if it was intentional or not, but I appreciated that she kept her tone at a whisper despite how mad she was.

"Listen, not right now, okay. I'll give you whatever you want just...please." Instantly, her eyes lit up at the possibilities and I knew my bank account was about to take a hit. I was willing to do anything if Farrah didn't find her though.

"I want a shopping spree on Michigan Ave.," she stated strongly. Without batting an eye, I nodded as I shoved her clothes into her chest and tried to push her toward the small closet in my office, but she stopped abruptly. "And a vacation with my girls, anywhere I wanna go." Clenching my jaw, I nodded once again, even though I really wanted to strangle her money hungry ass. She gave a gleeful squeal and damn near danced to the closet on her own. When she was finally closed inside, I shook off my nerves and pulled the door open for my wife. By now she was out of breath and wild eyed. Pushing past me, she threw herself into my office.

"Where is she? I know you have a whore in here some-where!" Dumbfounded by her behavior, I stood frozen as she ran around my desk and looked underneath it before moving to my ensuite. Since there were multiple places for her to check in the bathroom, I took the opportunity to usher Natasha, who was now fully dressed, out of the closet and out of my office. With her gone I could literally breath again as Farrah finally emerged and looked right at the closet like she was just noticing it. I stood back with my arms folded, almost pleased with how she was making a fool of herself.

"Farrah, this is getting ridiculous. You're causing a scene at my place of work and—"

"Fuck your place of work, De'Niko! You think I want to stick around for this type of embarrassment! My father was in Forbes, I don't need this shit! I don't need your cheating ass either!" She pointed at me, laughing maniacally, and began pacing the floor, instantly making me nervous. I hurried to close my office door in hopes that no one had heard her ranting already.

"You need to calm down," I told her sternly, even though I was slightly afraid of how erratic she was behaving. Since we'd been married, Farrah hadn't so much as raised her voice at me, no matter how mad she was. Not even when I'd sprung Kaliyah on her had she behaved in such a way. She'd merely stopped speaking to me, but after a conversation with my mother she eventually came around. Anytime I was caught cheating she allowed me to scheme my way back, and this time shouldn't have been any different, which was why I didn't understand the way she was going off.

"I don't *need* to do anything but call me a good divorce attorney! You, on the other hand, should probably call your parents." The sinister smirk on her face as she went to walk away told me that she was talking about something deeper than our shit, and I tried to grab her hand to stop her, but she snatched away.

"Fuck!" I shouted as she stormed out of my office just as Lynn came rushing in looking frantic.

"Mr. Black, I think you—"

"Not right now, Lynn!" It seemed like she had the worst possible timing, and the last thing I needed to be focusing on was something business related when my father's arrangement was about to go down the drain. Farrah had made many threats in our eight years of marriage, but I never feared her actually following through until a few minutes ago. I needed to call my parents immediately and I didn't want Lynn's worrisome ass in the room while I did.

"Sir, I really think you need to see this," she rambled, coming around my desk to where I was now sitting. I opened my mouth to object, but she slammed her hand on the wooden surface, shocking me momentarily. "No! This is important!"

Before I could dismiss her again, she began playing a video on her cellphone, and as soon as I heard Adore's voice I snatched it away. The first thing I noticed was how beautiful she looked despite the anguish on her face, and I took a moment to drink her in. My ears perked up when I heard my family's name though. I watched the full three-minute video, replaying it a few times before focusing in on the amount of likes, comments, and shares. Over one million people had liked the video, and a lot of the comments were attacking my family, which was the last thing I needed. I thought for sure we had her under lock and key with the contract, but obviously being around the likes of Heavy had caused some of his delinquency to rub off on her. Anger washed over me as she relayed all of our dirty secrets to the whole world. There were people in fucking Australia commenting about how terrible my family was! In addition to threats on our lives, there were actually some people giving her legal advice and offering to hook her up with a lawyer. Her connection to us had made it almost impossible to find legal representation in the city, but I wasn't sure we had the reach to stop outsiders from assisting her.

Feeling sick, I loosened my tie and wiped the sweat from my forehead as I realized this was what Farrah had been talking about. It was no wonder she'd walked out laughing, but she was just as involved as I was, maybe even more so. Her inability to give me a child of our own had been the number one reason why she agreed to stay and raise Kaliyah. The only problem with that was the older Kaliyah got the more she looked like her real mother, and that seemed to only remind her of my infidelity. I was sure she could feel the disconnect from the woman that was supposed to be her mother, so it wasn't hard for her to believe Adore when she said she was her actual mom. I could've kicked myself for letting that slip because it made her extremely curious. She'd been asking about Adore every day since they met and I always dismissed her, hoping she would eventually let it go.

My phone vibrating brought me back to the present, and I stiffened upon seeing my father's name on the screen. I contemplated not answering but knew that would only piss him off more. So, instead of sending him to voicemail I pressed accept.

"I'm going to kill that little bitch! Do you hear me! She's as good as dead!" he fumed, hanging up before I could even find the words to respond. Knowing the type of connections my father had instantly made me worried, and I prayed that Adore and her family went into hiding, because De'Niko Sr. was dead serious.

CHAPTER THIRTEEN

ISIS

I rolled my eyes at the sight of my baby daddy and continued bagging up the items for the customer I was checking out. He'd been blowing my phone up for days and I knew it was because he'd gotten the results like I had, but that didn't stop me from hitting ignore every time. After catching him with Carmise, I had less than nothing to say to him until the baby was born. I'd put a lot of faith in him only for that shit to blow up in my face, and I was officially done. Putting on a fake smile, I placed the last item in the bag.

"Okay, your total is $206.45," I said, surprised that my irritation wasn't evident in my voice.

"Oooh, that's not bad at all!" the girl squeaked, counting out a few bills and handing them over.

"Yeah girl, we aim to please." I put my focus on counting out the money and marking it to make sure it wasn't fake, before handing her the change along with her receipt. "Here you go, have a good day and come again."

"Oh, I'll definitely be back," she promised, turning to leave, and as soon as the door shut behind her I put my attention back on the inventory list I'd been working on before. I could feel Quay's eyes on me, but I kept my head down, hoping he'd get fed up and just leave. Unfortunately, that was too much like right.

"Ice, I know you see my ass standin' right here, man!" Somehow he'd moved from across the room and was right in front of me. I really wanted to continue ignoring him, but I knew he'd only show his ass.

"What do you want, Ja'Quay?" I sighed, never lifting my eyes from the papers in front of me.

"I got the results back." His voice softened, but I was unmoved by his attempt to be somewhat nice to me. It was too late for his ass to backpedal. He'd said and done everything he meant to say and do, and he needed to stand on that because I was going to. My mama always told me that an angry or drunk person will tell you how they really feel, so I fully believed he meant everything he'd been saying to me since the night he caught me at Bronx's house.

"Congratulations," I said smartly. "Is that all you wanted? Because I have work to finish around here." My heart pounded as he silently took me in, and I hated that regardless of how mad I was, he still had the ability to effect me. Unable to hold his gaze, I looked away, feeling like a goofy for not cowering.

"I wanted to come apologize to yo' stubborn ass. I was fucked up for comin' at you like that when I *know* you. I can admit when I'm wrong and even if we don't get this shit back right, I want us to at least be cordial for our baby." My eyes darted back to him and I folded my arms.

"Yep." My lips popped on the p as I tried to hold in my irritation. I honestly felt like for all he'd done I deserved more than a simple apology. He was acting like he'd only forgotten my birthday when he'd threatened me, pulled a gun on me a couple times, and fucked my neighbor.

"I know you know about Carmise, but on our unborn, that bitch was lying. That was the first time I ever fucked her ass, but it wasn't no kissin' or shit, and I damn sure ain't put my mouth on that hoe!" he exclaimed like he could read my mind, but nothing he said helped his case, and I was even more pissed that he'd put it on our baby.

"That's between y'all, just keep my baby out of it."

"That's what I'm tryna tell you, it ain't shit between us! I don't want that bitch! I don't even like her ass, I was just doin' that shit 'cause I was pissed off. It was some stupid shit knowing how crazy that bitch is, but I swear I ain't gone do shit like that no more."

"Again, that's your business whether you mess with her or not, Ja'Quay." I shrugged and could tell he was irritated by my response, but he only released a heavy sigh.

"Ayite man, call me if you need something. If not, I'll just drop in to check on you and shit."

"Okay, but droppin' in won't be necessary. I'll see you around and at the appointments if you still want to come to those."

"Man, didn't I just tell yo' ass—you know what, you got that, Ice." He sucked his teeth irritably before swaggering off. It felt like I could breath again once he was finally gone, but at the same time my heart hurt. I never would've thought we would be on such bad terms, especially after everything we'd been through, but Quay had done a lot of fucked-up things and I honestly didn't think we'd be able to bounce back.

A few hours later I was on my way home. Quay's little pop up had made it almost impossible to finish my work day, and I eventually allowed the thought of food and my bed to cause me to close up earlier than usual. I reasoned that I wasn't getting many customers anyway, so after stopping through Chipotle, I messaged Adore to come over to help me eat it and drove my ass home.

As soon as I pulled up, I rolled my eyes at the sight of Carmise's unemployed ass sitting on the porch with her friends. I'd done my best to avoid her since the night she was on her porch screaming about her and my baby daddy's sex life. She was too damn messy for me and although I really wanted to beat her ass, I had to think about my baby. I started to just pull off so I could avoid her ass altogether, but she wasn't about to run me off my block and think she won. So instead of going with my first mind, I snatched up my bag of food and exited my car.

"Ugh, this bitch," I heard as soon as I reached the sidewalk, followed by a bunch of laughter. *Lame ass bitch!* I thought, balling my fist and picking up speed so I wouldn't be tempted to fuck her up, but apparently my silence was taken as fear. "Bitches be walkin' around like they're all that and can't even keep their nigga in check. I be riding the shit out that nigga face," she bragged, sending her bird-brain friends into another fit of laughter.

"You wild bitch. How you end up gettin' Quay's mean ass? I tried to give him some pussy before and he straight up told me no. He said something about me smelling like BV. Like what the fuck even is that?" one of them said, sounding dumb as fuck.

"He got a point, hoe. I been told you to get that shit checked out. Your pussy gone fall off you keep avoiding the doctor like you do."

"Yeah, or yo' ass gone be single with rancid pussy like Isis over there."

I'd literally just made it to my door and had done a good

job of ignoring her so far, but even without a reaction she kept pushing. Now I was about to give her ass what she was asking for. Backtracking, I stepped down off my porch. "You wanna fight or something, 'cause I can't see why you're still talking shit after you already fucked my nigga. The dick wasn't enough, you want these hands too?"

All of a sudden, they all got quiet as hell and looked to a surprised Carmise. Recovering, she laughed nervously and tried to wave me off, but it was too late for that. She had been talking too much shit to be acting so scary. "Girl, ain't nobody bouta fight you. I was just—"

"Exactly, so keep my name out yo' scary ass mouth before you find my fist in it!" Pleased that she was thoroughly checked, I turned to head inside finally. Fucking around with her, my damn food was going to be cold and if it was, I was definitely gonna beat her ass. I was almost back to my stairs when I heard feet running up behind me. Quickly dropping my food down on grass, I turned around swinging with all my might and caught Carmise right in the eye. It was on from there. We swapped blows back and forth, but I gained the upper hand when she tripped over her own feet. I took the opportunity to jump on top of her and pummel her face. Her lip split and blood started pouring from her nose, but I didn't let up. Not only had she been talking shit, but she'd tried to snake me knowing that my hands were official.

"Get this bitch off me!" she screamed, trying to cover her face, but I wasn't letting up.

"I wish one of y'all bitches would touch her!" I heard Adore's voice and grinned. I'd forgotten all about her coming over, and while she was only one person, those bitches didn't move from where they were watching on the sidelines. That's why I was so surprised when I was yanked off of Carmise, but the familiar scent of Quay's Dior cologne let me know exactly who had saved her. His presence only pissed me off more though, and I instantly started fighting his stupid ass too.

"Aye man, calm the fuck down! What you on, Isis! Yo' ass pregnant!"

"Fuck you! This shit all your hoe ass fault!" I screeched, twisting until he finally released me. Panting, I pushed him away even further and snatched up my food while he stood there looking confused. "Help yo' funky ass bitch up!" Storming past him with Adore right on my trail, I went inside, leaving him to deal with Carmise and her friends.

"What the fuck happened, bestie?" Adore asked as soon as the door shut behind us.

"That stupid bitch tried to snake me when I was coming in, so I had to beat her ass." I shrugged, plopping down on my couch and opening up my food. The fight had only made me hungrier and the smell of my burrito through the foil had my stomach rumbling loud as hell.

"Oh, fuck that! I wished I would've known. I would've had you tag me in, hoe!" The irritation in her voice had me laughing, but as soon as I lifted my food to take a bite, I got pissed off all over again.

"That bitch made my food get cold!" Angry tears poured out of my eyes and I didn't know if it was the fight or my ruined food that had me so upset, but I was ready to go back out and fuck Carmise up some more.

CHAPTER FOURTEEN

QUAY

I really thought I was doing something, going up to Ice's store to apologize. Getting the results back to the DNA test had put shit into perspective for me and I realized I needed to make shit right with her. I wasn't expecting her to welcome me back with open arms after all of the shit I'd done, but her coldness only showed me how bad I'd fucked up. Figuring I'd slide back on her with something to show her how sorry I was, I stopped my jeweler and a flower shop, hoping that a couple gifts would prove to her just how sorry I was. But her ass wasn't at her store and when I called my OG, she said Adore was on her way to Isis's house, so I took a detour. Seeing her pregnant ass outside fighting on the lawn while my sister stood by daring somebody to jump in had me pissed off. I'd only just confirmed the baby was even mine and she was already risking its life to fight some irrelevant ass hoe.

As soon as she ran her little ass in the house, I turned my attention to Carmise and the Gross sisters as they struggled to help her dumb ass up off the ground. Walking past them, I lifted my shirt to reveal my gun and held a silencing finger to my lips. They seemed to get the message as fear crossed each of their faces as they dragged Carmise inside of her house. I couldn't front though, I still felt a way about her having access to Isis after the way she beat her ass, and I made a mental note to handle that shit soon.

Somewhat satisfied that shit was squashed and the police wouldn't be called, I ducked back into my car and pulled off. I had some business shit to take care of anyway. After partnering with Heavy my schedule had become extra tight, but my pockets were fat as ever. I appreciated that he trusted me enough to put me in a better position, and I tried to make sure I kept mistakes and shit to a minimum. Tossing the roses in the backseat, I turned around and placed the bag with her jewelry into the glove box.

It had been a minute since I'd checked in with Manny, so I decided to drop by the trap and see what he had going on, and as soon as I pulled up, I got pissed all over again. The porch was full of niggas shooting dice, smoking, and just hanging out. I real life blew my top seeing a whole crackhead out front smoking a glass dick in the grass, and I immediately pulled out my gun.

"Aye, get yo' ass the fuck from round here with that shit!" I barked, walking up on the crackhead first. Startled, he jumped so hard he dropped the pipe, prompting him to look up right into the barrel of my gun.

"My bad, youngblood!" He threw his hands up and ran off but quickly came back to snatch up his pipe. Irritated, I started to kick his ass in the back as he bent down but focused my attention on the rowdy niggas on the porch instead. None of them had taken notice of my arrival, so I was able to easily make my way up the stairs and into the middle of their dice game where Manny was crouched dead center.

"Aye, what the fuck—" He hopped up, gripping his gun in

one hand and his money in the other, but once his eyes landed on me, he nervously laughed, tucking his gun back in his waist. "Oh damn, my bad, bro. What's up?"

"Y'all niggas gotta get the fuck on, and you other muhfuckas need to get back to work!" I ordered, ignoring Manny entirely. Knowing exactly what I was about, they all grabbed their shit and either disappeared inside the house or slinked off the porch. Once the last nigga left the property, I turned my attention back on Manny, who stood there scratching his head like none of this was his doing. "What's up?" I grit, motioning around the dirty ass porch. "What the fuck you got goin' on, nigga? You know this ain't how we do shit! You might as well call the jakes on yo' damn self!" I was trying to keep it cool, but I really wanted to shoot his ass in the foot or something.

"Man, it ain't that deep, wasn't even that many muhfuckas over here for real." His dismissive tone in addition to the shit I'd already dealt with at Isis's crib had my nostrils flaring, and I shoved his real goofy ass in the chest, sending him stumbling back a few feet.

"Fuck you talkin' bout, it was a whole crackhead out here smoking in the yard, nigga! You think you bouta fuck this shit up for me, you dumb as hell! I'll kill yo' ass before I get locked up behind yo' bullshit!" I told him, not giving a fuck about how he took it. I was dead ass serious too, and it was obvious that he knew it as he glared at me with his face balled up.

"You threatenin' me, nigga? Yo' fuckin' day one?" he huffed in disbelief and shook his head. "You really lettin' that shit with Heavy go to yo' muhfuckin' head, bro. You—"

"Yo, you suspended, I ain't bouta be sittin' here arguin' with yo' goofy ass like you my bitch or somethin'." I pulled my phone out to call Rock or Jay over to take his place until I figured out whether he was going to get his spot back. "Take yo' ass home until further notice."

"Nigga, this ain't no nine to five, you can't suspend me!" he fumed, unmoving, but I wasn't about to engage with his ass. Ignoring him, I put the phone up to my ear and quickly filled Jay in on what was going on, while Manny talked shit in the background. When he finally realized I wasn't changing my mind, he stomped off like a bitch, bumping my shoulder on the way. I let him have that since he was clearly in his feelings, and waited until his car disappeared off the block before going inside so I could get those niggas together too.

A few days later, I prepared to link with Heavy but quickly had to reroute when my mama and sister started blowing my phone up with back-to-back texts. They were both informing me that Isis had been taken to the hospital because she was bleeding, and I headed straight up there. I already knew it had something to do with her stupid ass fighting Carmise recently, and as soon as I made sure my baby was straight, I was going to curse her the fuck out.

When I pulled up to Rush Hospital, I gave them Isis's name and was quickly given access to the emergency room area. She was in one of the first rooms, and as soon as I entered, she gave my mama and sister dirty looks.

"Ain't no point lookin' at them, you better hope ain't shit wrong with my baby 'cause of that catty ass fight," I warned sternly, stepping into the tight room.

"First of all, it clearly wasn't the fight because that bitch didn't even touch me once. It's probably stress from yo' ass more than anything!" She rolled her eyes and placed her hands on her small belly, instantly shutting me up. The last thing I was trying to do was upset her even more while she was in the hospital, so I was going to hold off on bothering her at least until she was given a clean bill of health.

"The doctor been in yet?" I quickly changed the subject.

"She was in a little bit ago to let us know what tests they're running. We haven't gotten any results back yet though." Adore barely looked up from her phone to tell me. Ever since her video had gone viral, she'd been glued to that shit. Tons of lawyers and other people had been offering their services to her and they'd been going through trying to find the best fit. I couldn't lie, I was happy she was finally getting some help with her case for custody of Kaliyah. The Blacks had already made it almost impossible for her to come out on top, so to see their name getting drug through the mud and people seeing them for the fucked-up individuals they were was karma at its finest.

"Y'all can head out if y'all got something to do. I'ma stay up here until they discharge her," I said, dropping into the only free chair in the room.

"Nah, I can stay for a while, me and Isis were supposed to be going to eat anyway." Adore waved me off while my mama took the opportunity to gather her things.

"Okay, well, I picked up a shift so I'm gonna go take a little nap. Y'all let me know what they say." She gave us all hugs and was gone. I made myself comfortable and half listened to the TV as I returned a few texts, being careful not to say too much to Isis besides asking her ornery ass if she wanted or needed anything. She denied each of my attempts to be nice and I finally just left her alone. Thankfully, Dr. Smith came into the room a short time later, but her expression was grim as hell, instantly putting me on high alert.

"What's up, Doc, is the baby okay?" I quizzed, ready to tear shit up if something was wrong with my little one. Before answering, she gave Isis a questioning look.

"Is it alright to speak freely?" That shit had me sitting up in my chair. I didn't know how shit worked between women and their doctors, but off top, I felt like I should be privy to everything pertaining to my blood. Even after Isis nodded and gave her the okay, I was still on edge. "Well, right now, you seem to be stable. However, I'm going to have to put you on bed rest for the remainder of your pregnancy because you almost lost the baby today. Between your stress level and the amount of scar tissue from your previous termination, it will be difficult to ensure the safety of the baby unless you take it easy, and I mean all the way easy. No standing for longer than thirty minutes at a time. Your diet should also change to a much healthier one since less sugar and fats aid in overall wellbeing. I'm also going to have you coming to see me every week so I can keep a closer eye on you, and in the meantime, I would say to stay stress free. No unnecessary arguing or—"

"Termination?" I finally interrupted since that word had been bothering me well after she'd said it. Once again, Dr. Smith looked to Isis and so did I. I didn't care who explained that shit as long as somebody explained it. Isis swallowed hard and began twisting her fingers nervously, so I brought my eyes back to the doctor.

"A termination is when one undergoes an abortion—" she started to explain, but I cut her ass off again.

"When the fuck you had an abortion, Ice?" I glared at my baby mama, unfazed by the tears misting in her eyes.

"It was a couple of years ago. I—we weren't ready for a baby, so I made the best decision for us. I—"

"You just got all kinds of secrets, huh?" I cut her off with a sarcastic laugh. "How you gone tell me what the fuck I was ready for!" I barked, standing to my feet, mugging her goofy ass. Adore immediately stood too, trying to defuse the situation,, but it wasn't much she could say at this point to help her lying ass friend out.

"You weren't even ready to settle down, how the fuck was I supposed to know if you wouldn't just leave me stuck raising a baby on my own while you ran the streets fuckin' everything with legs!" she screamed back as tears flooded her face.

"That ain't got shit to do with a baby! My baby! You're selfish as fuck for this shit bro, on my mama!" Instead of arguing with me, she buried her face in her hands as the doctor advised me to leave, but I was already ahead of her. Just the little bit of arguing we'd just done could've potentially harmed the baby, and I didn't need that shit on my conscience.

CHAPTER FIFTEEN
ADORE

It took a long ass time to finally get Isis calmed down after Quay left, and it had a lot to do with whatever they put in her IV. By the time they finally discharged her she was stoic, but she was no longer crying hysterically. I kept my questions to myself, knowing that now all she really needed was a friend. I'd was still reeling from finding out that she'd been pregnant before and while I could understand where my brother was coming from, I also could see her point of view. Especially when she had a front row seat to the fuckery I dealt with upon getting pregnant with Kaliyah. Still, I texted Quay to make sure he was okay, because I'd never seen him so hurt. He didn't message back right away, but I figured he was just too mad so I was going to let him have that. In the meantime, I helped Isis out of the emergency room and immediately sighed heavily when I realized she'd been the one to drive us there. With my mama at work and Quay in the wind, the only other person I could call was Heavy. And just like any other time, he answered right away. As soon as his voice came over the line, I felt that fluttering in my stomach. It was almost childish the way I lit up over him, but I liked how he made me feel and I hoped he didn't do anything to change it.

As promised, Heavy pulled up about twenty minutes later and helped me get Isis into the back seat while some other dude named Jarvis got her keys so he could follow us in her car. "Yo' ass really needs to learn how to drive, man," he cracked, leaning across the console and giving me a bunch of quick kisses that had me wanting more despite him talking shit.

"Not you soundin' like my mama." Pretending to pout, I folded my arms and went to move away, only for him to pull me right back.

"Stop it. If you're tired of hearing about it then do something about it. Matter fact, I'm gone take you for yo' first lesson tomorrow." Determination had me agreeing with a goofy grin on my face. I didn't know the first thing about controlling a car, but I was sure that Heavy would be a good teacher.

"Awwwww, y'all so cute!" Isis gushed from the back seat before starting to cry again. Heavy's forehead bunched and he peered at us both, but I only shook my head and mouthed that it was a long story. Reaching into the back seat, I pet her leg encouragingly.

"It's okay, boo. You wanna stop and grab some food on the way home?" The question had her drying her eyes with a nod as she ran down a list of things from McDonald's of all places. My little niece or nephew had her all over the place because she usually didn't even like McDonald's, but I didn't hesitate to direct Heavy to head to the nearest location.

A short time later she sat in the back pigging out as we pulled up to her apartment, and my jaw dropped at the sight of a huge U-Haul parked on her lawn. Her door was wide open and a handful of niggas moved in and out, loading up the truck with her things. Isis, who hadn't noticed right away, instantly cursed around a mouthful of food. Heavy barely had a chance to stop the car before she jumped out and was running across the grass. Already knowing that I was about to hop out too, he dropped the gear in park and followed me up with his gun in hand.

We all stopped in our tracks when Quay stepped out onto the porch casually eating a bag of Flamin' Hots. "What the fuck is yo' crazy ass doin', Quay?" Isis shouted, rushing up the stairs.

"You trippin', you supposed to be taking it easy but you out here running and yelling and shit!" he chastised her. "Yo' doctor said you need to be on bed rest, so you bouta move in with me so I can make sure you do what you're supposed to. Plus, I can keep an eye on yo' sneaky ass. Any questions?" Horror covered my girl's face and she slowly backed away from him like she really thought his ass was crazy.

"No!"

"No questions? Good," he questioned, pouring more chips in his mouth, and she sucked her teeth irritably.

"No, I'm not moving, muhfucka! Tell these niggas to bring my shit right back in here!" Her outburst had the movers pausing and looking to Quay, unsure of what they should do. Ignoring her, he snapped his fingers for them to keep going.

"Keep doin' what the fuck I paid y'all to." Isis stomped and let out a groan as they continued to move her things. "Go wait in the car, they're almost done and you ain't supposed to be standing this long anyway."

"*Quay!*" she whined and began bawling again. Instead of putting a stop to this madness this fool finished his chips, balled up the bag, and tossed it before swooping her off her feet. He nodded to Heavy as he passed us, carrying her to his truck that I hadn't even noticed was out there.

"This nigga crazy." Heavy shook his head and tucked his gun back in his waist. "Let's go before his ass try to have us movin' shit too," he joked, reaching for my hand. I had to admit my family was crazy as hell, but somehow it worked for them. Even as we made our way back to Heavy's car, I could see my brother standing in the passenger door embracing Isis in an attempt to calm her down. Shaking my head, I made a mental note to call her later and make sure she was okay as we pulled off. "You tryna stay with me tonight?" he asked, surprising the fuck out of me. Heavy was never too forward, and while I liked his usual pace I couldn't deny how bad I'd been wanting to actually sleep with him. Blushing, I agreed and settled back into my seat as I imagined how the night would go.

I didn't realize how draining the day had been though, until Heavy woke me up out of a semi-deep slumber. Rubbing my eyes, I followed him inside his house, already kind of knowing my way around since I'd been there a couple of times. "I'm gone set you up in the guest room if that's cool?" That had me confused as fuck because I thought the whole point of staying the night with somebody meant actually stay *with* them. I was completely out of my element when it came to asking for what I wanted sexually, and I tried to think of what Isis would tell me to say without sounding crazy.

"I, um, I'd rather sleep with you though." I immediately chastised myself for sounding so unsure, and the baffled look on Heavy's face only made me feel more embarrassed. "I mean, it's ok, I can sleep in the guest room." I pressed my lips together to stop myself from saying anything else awkwardly and completely avoided eye contact. Heavy's silence was deafening even though I could feel his eyes on me. I was able to finally release the breath I'd been holding when he led me upstairs. That is until we passed up every other room for the master suite.

"I thought..?"

"You don't have to feel pressured to sleep in here, baby. I can still go hook up the guest room for you if that's what you really want." He shrugged, brushing his hand down his waves, and I bit back a squeal as I threw my body into him. I could tell he was caught off guard, but he quickly recovered, wrapping his arms around my slim waist and pressing his lips against mine. Our kissing grew deeper, hungrier as his tongue explored my mouth, making me whimper in longing. I could already feel my panties getting wet as my center spasmed, anticipating his touch. With ease he lifted me off my feet, gripping the bottom of my thighs as I wrapped myself around his slim but muscular frame. I was so into the way he was devouring my lips that I didn't realize he had walked us into his master bath until he sat me on the sink. That's when he paused long enough to start the shower. He had one of the fancy digital ones so I knew it was going to feel amazing. After getting the temperature set right and stripping out of his sweatshirt, he came back to stand between my legs. His warm hands glided underneath my T-shirt, pulling it over my head and exposing the black bra underneath. I had no idea what he was doing to me, but it felt like his hands were everywhere. Gripping my breasts, my neck, even slipping down the front of my leggings. I instantly moaned when he came into contact with my wetness.

"Can I taste you?" His voice was husky as he asked, staring deeply into my eyes. Panting with anticipation, I nodded and released a breathy yes, giving him the green light. He took his time dropping wet kisses down my body until he was face to face with my sex, driving me wild in the process. Thirsty, I assisted him in sliding my leggings and panties down until they were completely off. It had to be the sexiest thing I'd ever witnessed to see him staring straight at my pussy in hunger before gently spreading my slippery lips.

"Oh my! Baaaaby!" I cried when he latched onto my clit. Considering I'd only had one other partner in my life, Heavy was definitely the better of the two. I grinded against his face as he tongue kissed my pussy. Moaning, he slipped his middle finger inside me and I instantly tightened around him.

"Pussy so fucking good," he grunted, pushing my legs open wider. I could already feel my body begin to tingle, letting me know my orgasm was fast approaching, and my breathing picked up.

"Dominique! I-I'm bouta cuuum!" It was like he already knew it was coming and went even harder, stroking my g-spot and simultaneously sucking my clit until I exploded.

"Good girl." He looked up at me and sucked my juices off his finger. My body was still shaking as he licked me clean. I'd never had an orgasm so mind blowing and I was almost sure I couldn't take any more pleasure, especially when Heavy was fully undressed and standing before me with three fucking legs. He grinned cockily as my eyes widened, darting between him and the monster he called a dick. Before I could open my mouth to ask him where he planned to put that thing, he was kissing me as he lifted my now tense body and carried me into the shower. I could already feel him poking at my opening, but his tongue wrestling with mine had me throbbing once again. Pressing my back against the warm tile, he glided himself between my silky folds, putting me on the verge of another orgasm.

"It's been a while, so be easy," I pleaded, wrapping my arms around his neck tightly.

"Look at me." The order was so commanding that despite my embarrassment I did as he said, staring down at him through my lashes. "Don't worry, I got you." He firmly held my gaze and eased the head in. Just that little bit had my face scrunching in pain, but I pushed through. I could feel him stretching me open and I dug my nails in his back as he talked to me lowly, telling me to try and relax. He kissed me passionately and continued working his way inside me until I was overcome with more pleasure than pain.

"Mmmm," I moaned.

"You're choking the fuck out my dick, baby, damn!" Heavy tore his lips away from mine and sucked my chin before moving down to my neck. Between him talking nasty, his mouth all over me, and his dick constantly hitting my g-spot, I was already on the verge of another orgasm. "You ready to nut again?" he asked, gripping my ass in both hands.

"Ye-yessss! Yeeessss, I'm ready!"

"Let me feel it then." As if my body was already under his full control, my walls began contracting and I felt a gush of wetness erupt from inside me. "Oh, she a fuckin' squirter! You bouta catch this nut like a good girl, bae?" I hardly had any authority over my body at this point, but somehow, I managed to nod, squealing out a loud yes as I felt him begin to swell and pulse. His strokes became shorter and harder before he finally growled in my ear.

My legs were like noodles by the time Heavy put me onto my feet, and he grinned down at me proudly, dropping another kiss on my lips. Scared to move, I stayed pressed up against the shower wall while he grabbed the soap and a couple of towels from a clear cabinet built into the wall. Reaching out for me, he made light work of washing me from head to toe while I stood there and tried not to fall asleep. After washing himself off, he wrapped me up in a huge dry towel that reached my calves and led me to his comfortable looking bed. I went to lay down while he found us something to sleep in, and the last thing I remember before my eyes drifted closed was him disappearing inside his walk-in closet.

CHAPTER SIXTEEN
HEAVY

I woke up the next morning to Adore pressed against me and couldn't stop myself from smiling as I kissed her forehead. As bad as I wanted to bury myself inside her again, I had some shit to take care of. Slowly easing out from under her, I pulled the blanket over her and climbed out of bed. I ducked into the bathroom to piss and handle my hygiene before grabbing my cell and quietly leaving the room. Adore didn't know it, but I'd invited her over for a reason and it had nothing to do with pussy. I'd gotten first-hand information that Black's bitch ass had tried to put a price on Adore's head. With the governor pushing to have him suspended pending an investigation, I guess he felt like he didn't have shit to lose. What he didn't bank on was me ensuring that no harm came to her, even if I had to pay double what he had. As I descended the stairs, the first person I called was John. I already knew that her mama was working overnight, so I had him keeping an eye on her until I heard back about the hit being rejected.

"Yo, everything good on yo' end?" I cut straight to the

chase as I entered the kitchen and began pulling out every-thing I'd need for a simple breakfast.

"Yeah boss, she just made it home not too long ago and there hasn't been any movement so far," he informed me, and I could hear him stifling a yawn, instantly making me feel bad. No doubt I used him a lot when it came to watching because that was his main job, but I knew he was probably tired from having worked the last twenty-four hours.

"Ayite, I'ma have Jarvis come swap positions so you can get some rest until I fill Quay in on what's going on."

"Bet."

Hanging up with him, I called Jarvis with his new orders as I moved about the kitchen hooking up a quick omelet and some bacon for Adore when she finally woke up. Once I was finished, I tried Quay's phone, only for it to go to ring until the voicemail picked up. Last night hadn't been a good time to tell him about what was going on, but I also didn't want to wait too long before informing him of the potential threat to his sister, even though she had nothing to worry about as long as she was with me.

"Oooooh, you cook too?" I heard behind me and turned to see Adore leaned up against my refrigerator in only one of my t-shirts. Setting down my phone and her plate, I immediately reached for her, noting the slight limp in her walk with a smirk.

"We aim to please," I teased, kissing her pouty lips as she stopped in front of me. "You sleep good?" Gripping a handful of her ass, I pulled her closer so her body was flush up against mine.

"Did I? Your bed feels like a whole ass cloud! I almost didn't even want to get out of it, but I missed you." Sighing, she rubbed her hands along my back and looked up at me with puckered lips, instantly making my dick jump in my shorts. Adore definitely had the type of pussy that made a nigga not want to leave the bed. "Nope, you keep that thing to yourself!" she giggled, trying to move, but I pulled her right back, turning so that she was trapped between me and the island.

"This *your* dick, girl, I'm just tryna share it with you." I was only half joking, because I was already growing hard just being so close to her fine ass. She shuddered as I slipped my hand under her shirt, quickly finding her center, and just like I expected, she was wet. My mouth watered as I considered lifting her ass onto the island and eating her pussy for breakfast, when the doorbell rang. "Fuck!"

"Saved by the bell." Adore's lame ass giggled and slipped out from under me while I cursed out whoever was at the door in my head. She was already sitting on one of the barstools and cutting into her food, smirking at me when the bell rang again, this time with more urgency. Making a quick stop by the sink, I washed and dried my hands and made my way to answer the door. I was prepared to curse somebody the fuck out, but my irritation instantly turned to alarm at the sight of Kay Kay and her mama. I'd completely forgotten that I was supposed to be driving her to school. Backing away from the door, I ran a hand down my face and took a deep breath to try and figure out a way out of this. While Kay Kay liked Adore, she wasn't used to seeing any woman in our home, and I didn't know how she'd act if she caught her half naked in our kitchen.

I could hear her whining about how long I was taking and shrugged off my worry. It was too late to do shit about it now. I'd just have to see how she reacted if I explained Adore's presence first. Before I could stop myself, I went ahead and pulled the door open. She immediately looked at me suspiciously, but it could've very well been my paranoia.

"Daddy, what took you so long?" she huffed, stomping inside.

"My bad, baby, I was cooking something and couldn't leave it on the stove." The lie rolled off my tongue, and the mention of food had her eyes lighting up while Sha'ron looked at me curiously.

"Sorry, I tried to call and remind you but..." her voice trailed off and she looked off uncomfortably.

"It's cool, I got her," I said dryly, shutting the door in her face. That was the nicest response I had for her, and even though I tried not to disrespect her in front of our daughter, I also wasn't going to be unnecessarily nice either. She was lucky I was even speaking to her snake ass.

"I hope you made enough for me!" Kay Kay shouted, already taking off for the kitchen, and I quickly followed, like my presence would stop the awkward interaction. "Adore!" I heard her exclaim right before I rounded the corner to see her run up to a stunned Adore.

"He-heeey, baby!" She hugged Kay Kay back and raised her brows at me over her head.

"My bad, I forgot she was coming," I mouthed, lifting my plate so I could give it to her since I'd only made enough for two.

"Daddy, why didn't you tell me Adore was here?" my nosy ass baby asked, finally pulling away and giving me an accusing glare.

"We got in late, baby, you were in bed and asleep for school at eleven at night." Setting her plate on the island next to Adore, I gave her a knowing look. I'd caught her staying up late a few times, on her tablet, and I knew she wasn't just reserving that behavior for my house because my mama had mentioned it too.

"Riiiiiight." Dropping the subject, she slinked over to her stool and began filling her mouth while I poured her some Sunny D.

"Riiiiiight."

"Can Adore come with you to drop me off?" she wanted to know, and I quickly shot the question back, raising a brow at Adore.

"You gotta ask her if she wants to come, Kay Kay. I'm sure she doesn't want to wait around in line to—"

"Actually, I'd love to come," Adore cut me off with a smirk. I couldn't help but agree then as they giggled and talked amongst each other in hushed tones.

"I guess we're all driving to school then. You're gonna need on more than that gown though," I teased, pointing to my shirt and causing Kay Kay to smack her lips, tilting her little head.

"That's not a gown, that's your shirt, Daddy." She stayed calling me out, but I was going to let her have that because I didn't want her to ask me why Adore had on my shirt. Instead, I left them to eat while I went to shower and throw on some clothes so I could take her talkative ass to school.

———

After dropping Kay Kay off at school, I stalled trying to keep Adore at the house with me since she was off. It didn't take much but bribing her with more food and dick, which both had her knocked out again by noon. That worked perfect for me, keeping her out of my hair for a while so I could get in contact with a few people and ensure her and her family's safety. Knowing my connection to Adore and how our connection to each other would make him look bad, Mayor Black had been avoiding my calls. I wouldn't hesitate to pull up on him, as soon as I had the time, but if I did it would get ugly, and I was sure he didn't want that. The only thing saving him was his position and the fact that Adore would be the number one suspect. My phone ringing snapped me out of my thoughts, and I hurried to answer once I saw Quay's name on the screen.

"Nigga, where the fuck you been?" I hissed as soon as the call connected.

"Why everything so urgent with yo' ass? Did you see the shit I was tied up with last night, nigga? It took forever to get her shit straightened out after them goofy ass muhfuckas loaded that truck up all sloppy! I'm up now though, what's up?"

"I need you to get over to my crib ASAP, it's important," I let him know, checking to make sure Adore wasn't up and moving around. He hesitated briefly before agreeing, and I ran down my address to him. After we got off the phone, I stayed on the couch watching TV until he arrived. It wasn't long before he pulled up and let me know he was outside.

"What's up, I ain't got too long to be gone before Isis wakes her worrisome ass up," he said, stepping into the foyer, and I immediately filled him in on what was going on. Anger washed over his face at the news that De'Niko had a price on Adore's head. "Why the fuck you ain't tell me this on the phone so I could've went there first?"

"That ain't some shit to say over the phone. Besides, do you really think I'd take her ass home knowing that nigga got a hit out on her? I got Adore here with me and somebody is watching y'all's mama. I done had a tail on her since last night when I found out." That information calmed him down slightly, but I could tell he was still worried as fuck.

"Why can't we just take his ass out and just eliminate the problem all together? I been waiting to shoot his ass anyway, and if he tryna kill my sister it's only right I lay his ass down first." A gasp sounding behind me stopped me from explaining why it would be bad to kill him right then or anytime soon for that matter, and my eyes shut with a sigh.

"Who's trying to kill me?"

CHAPTER SEVENTEEN
QUAY

Looking up at my sister at the top of the stairs, I hurried to say, "Yo' baby daddy people." Confusion covered her face as Heavy mugged me for snitching, but that shit didn't faze me at all. My biggest concern was protecting her from my niece's crooked ass relatives.

"What the fuck? Is he for real, Dominique!" she quizzed, racing down the stairs.

"Yeah but—"

"*Yeah*?" she gasped, cutting him off. "When did you find this out?"

"Last night on the way to take Isis home, I—"

"Wait, wait, wait. De'Niko Sr. is trying to kill me and you knew about it all this time, but thought it'd be better to fuck than tell me my life is in jeopardy?"

"Whoa, TMI bro! What the fuck you on!" I grumbled, backing away with my hands up. It went without saying that the two were probably fucking, but I wasn't trying to hear that shit. Sucking her teeth, she waved me off.

"Shut up, Ja'Quay! You're literally worried about the wrong

shit right now," she scoffed, and I resisted the urge to snap back on her ass, but I let her make it since she was getting some wild news.

"Ayite, I did find out last night and maybe I should've told you that shit right then, but the whole reason I brought you here was to keep yo' ass safe! Ain't that what I said last night that I wasn't tryna bring you here to fuck?" He lowered his voice and took a couple steps toward her, and as serious as the situation was I couldn't help watching them with my face scrunched up. "I know you're scared and shit, but you gotta know that I been doin' everything I could to keep yo' ass alive. Why you think you been here all day? I ain't let you outta my sight and I got somebody watchin' yo' OG too just to cover all the bases."

"Hold up, that nigga got a hit out on my mama too? I knew I shoulda killed his ass when I had the chance!" I interjected, growing more amped at the news. Even Adore's ears perked up at the question, looking at him with wide eyes. Sighing, Heavy shook his head.

"Not that I know of, but with the publicity surrounding them from the TikTok video, he can't just have her get shot or no shit. It'd have to be more low key, like an accident so the shit don't trace back to him. Same with Adore, it ain't shit *we* can do to his ass without it looking like something she orchestrated."

"Damn, well we gotta do something. We can't let his ass just skate for this shit," I mused, pissed that the attention Adore was getting had pushed us into a corner.

"I ain't sure yet what we can do, but I'm tryna work something out right now. Just give me a couple days to see what I can come up with." I studied him silently for a few seconds before nodding and shaking up with him.

"Ayite, keep me updated. I'm bouta go grab my OG and

head back to the crib to make sure this girl ain't tried to dip out since I'm not there."

"Not you thinkin' you bouta leave me! I'm comin' to see my mama too!" Adore fussed, already trying to run and grab her shoes from by the door.

"Nah sis, it's safer for you to stay with the big homie for right now. At least until we can get a better understanding of what's going on. I can't watch you, my mama, and Isis ole bedridden ass," I tried to joke, but judging from the irritation on her face it did nothing to put her at ease. I could understand her worry, but at the same time, sticking close to Heavy was her best option. Besides that, I wasn't trying to be stuck in a house with all their worrisome asses with the shit that was going on. I'd fuck around and go crazy.

"I got her man, gon' head." Heavy stepped up, wrapping an arm around her waist, and I paused just before stepping out the door.

"I'ma hold you to that, bro. Keep my sister safe." Giving him a warning look, I set out to go pick up my mama. She was coming out to grab the mail when I pulled up, and she waited while I got out, greeting me with a smile.

"Hey, crazy ass boy, I been callin' you and yo' sister all morning. Shit, I was bouta slide on y'all asses!" she chuckled, giving me a kiss on the cheek once I made it up the porch to her. I wasn't trying to alarm her, but paranoia had me looking around for anything out of place until they landed on the black town car that was parked a few houses down and across the street. The driver gave me a salute to let me know he was Heavy's man, and I ushered her inside. She was rambling on about her night at work and asking me questions about how Isis was doing.

"Ice good, Ma, but I need you to come with me. Pack a bag for a couple days—"

"What you mean come with you? I most certainly ain't, and what about Adore, where is she at? Should I be worried? What the fuck I'm talkin' 'bout, of course I should be worried!" she sighed, pinching the bridge of her nose like I was getting on her nerves.

"Niko put a hit out on Adore because of the attention from the TikTok video. She straight right now, she put up with Heavy until we figure this shit out, but until then I need you to stay with me." My breakdown of the situation only had her looking at me crazy as hell.

"Wait, that nigga did what! Oh, hell naw, 'cause he got my baby fucked up!" she snapped, clapping her hands with each word, just like Isis would do if she was pissed off. I allowed her to get her shit off for a few before finally stopping her rant.

"Ma, chill man, you talkin' crazy and we need to be leaving like right now. Besides, I got Isis at the crib and I gotta make sure she stay her lil' ass in the bed like the doctor told her to." This was the second time I'd said I needed to get back to Ice and it had me feeling the need to call her sneaky ass. Since she'd gotten pregnant, I'd been finding out all her secrets and it had me questioning a lot of shit about her. Still, I couldn't wash my hands of her completely. Mainly because she was carrying my baby, but also because I had a soft spot for her that gave her more leeway than any other woman could ever get from me. That's why as mad as I was, I brought her to my crib so I could ensure nothing happened to my baby, and to try to get us back on the same page.

"Who the fuck you think you yellin' at? And don't tell me no fuckin' chill! You know what, let me go call my baby before I have to go upside yo' damn head!" She walked off talking shit while I pulled out my phone to call Isis. Her phone rang a couple of times before going to voicemail, letting me know she'd ignored me. The same thing happened when I called her back and instantly pissed me off. I was about to call her ass again when my mama came strolling down the stairs with an overnight bag and her phone pressed against her ear, talking loudly. From her end I could tell she was talking to my sister as she handed me her bag. Shoving my phone in my pocket, I carried her shit out to the car while she locked up. Her talkative ass stayed on the phone with Adore the whole way to my crib, only ending the call once I pulled into my driveway.

The first thing I saw when we entered the house was Isis sitting on the couch wide awake, eating carrots and ranch with her phone right next to her as she watched TV. "You ain't see me callin' yo' ass!" I fussed, stalking over to her with my mama right on my heels.

"Hey Ma, what you doin' over here?" she ignored me, speaking only to my mama, who plopped down next to her. I instantly shook my head, so she knew not to tell her the real reason she was there in an effort to keep her stress down as much as possible. Just from her facial expression alone, I knew she didn't like that shit but thankfully, she kept it to herself.

"Oh, I came to make y'all something to eat. You know I gotta keep my grandbaby fed." That had Isis dancing in her seat happily, and my mama rolled her eyes then reached to rub her little pudge. Them ganging up on me was exactly the reason I didn't want to add Adore's ass to the mix.

"Ignore me all you want, but don't sit yo' ass down here all day. You know the doctor said only twenty minutes out of bed. Keep playin' with me, I'ma hire a nurse to sit with yo' ass for the next six months," I warned and headed upstairs to get a little more sleep before starting my day. I felt much better with my OG there monitoring her in my absence. At least I'd know she wasn't going to disappear while I was asleep. When I made it upstairs I fell straight across the bed and was knocked out.

I was up again a couple hours later to do my pickups, but

before I could even leave the house Rock was messaging me to meet him at the trap. It took me about twenty minutes to handle my hygiene and throw on some sweats. My mama had the whole crib smelling good, and I went in search of my baby mama since she wasn't in the bed like I told her ass to be.

Hearing the TV in one of the guest rooms led me there, and I breathed a sigh of relief seeing Isis sitting up in bed with a big ass fruit bowl in her lap. As soon as she saw me it was me, her eyes narrowed evilly.

"I ain't tryna irritate you, I do appreciate you takin' you and the baby's health seriously though. I'm bouta make a couple runs, do you want something while I'm out?" Her mouth hung open, not having expected me to come at her like that, and I resisted the urge to take a picture of the shock on her face. She snapped her lips together, clearly at a loss for words before shrugging.

"I'd like more Fiji water if you can."

"I got you," I let her know before shutting her door back.

After letting my OG know I'd be back in a bit, I locked up and jumped in my car. My first stop was going to be to see Rock since that was the closest. As soon as I pulled up, I was pleased to see the front porch and yard clear of clucks and random ass niggas. Rock always stayed on his business, and I appreciated him keeping niggas in check. Checking the time, I realized I was behind schedule, so I needed to put a little rush on this meeting.

I took the stairs two at a time and did a special knock so they knew it was me. I wasn't even surprised when Rock was the one who answered, stepping out and locking the door back behind us.

"What up, bro?"

"Shit, just tryna make it," I said, shaking up with him.

"On my soul, that's all a nigga can do." He looked up and

down the dark street, before rubbing his hands together. "Anyway, I had you stop through 'cause that nigga Manny done lost it. He pissed about Jay taking his spot. If he ain't complainin' 'bout that shit then he talking about you fuckin' with Heavy so tough. Real bitch nigga shit," he scoffed, spitting off the side of the porch. My face instantly balled up hearing that shit. Not only because I thought I'd looked out for him, but I hadn't detected no hater shit on his part. My first thought was to go smoke his ass off GP, but it was only right I try to get to the root of the issue before killing my homie. I thanked Rock for the information with my next move heavy on my mind as I went to pick up Isis's water.

CHAPTER EIGHTEEN
ISIS

I t had been a couple weeks since I'd moved into Quay's house and I was bored as hell. I was used to working and meeting people. Sitting in the house cooped up was not something I wanted to do, and it didn't help that I hadn't seen much of my bestie either. Adore had been working overtime at the diner and baking shit on the side. When she wasn't doing that she was meeting with the lawyer she'd finally obtained since her story had gone viral. People were finally looking at the Black family under a microscope and that's exactly what they deserved. I could only hope and pray that they got jail time for one of the crimes I was sure they'd committed. Niko's daddy had already been suspended pending an investigation and it would serve his ass right to be terminated publicly.

I was really excited for my girl and slightly pissed that after all our brainstorming a damn angry TikTok rant had been the golden ticket. As much as I loved the app, I would've been told her to put her story out there. Either way, I was happy that she was finally getting somewhere in her fight for Kaliyah, I just wished I was there to see it and not watching it through my phone.

I heard heavy footsteps coming up the stairs and instantly tucked the junk food I'd been eating under my pillow. His fresh scent entered before he did, and by the time Quay stuck his head in the door I was eating the apple slices I'd brought up there as a decoy. The pleased grin on his face when he saw me had me feeling just a little bad about lying, but if he and Dr. Smith thought I was about to spend the rest of my pregnancy on bed rest *and* a rabbit diet, then they were both crazy as hell.

"Aye, I was just comin' to let you know I was back. You feelin' ok? How my mini me doin'?" Every time he mentioned the baby he lit up with pride and it was the cutest shit ever. It almost made me not as angry with him for forcing me to move...almost.

"We're good, Quay, it ain't like we can go anywhere," I said smartly and rolled my eyes. I might have thought the attention was kind of cute but I still wasn't letting his ass off the hook. Sighing, he stepped completely in the room and shut the door behind him.

"I know you don't like this shit, but all I'm tryna do is make sure you and my baby straight. I don't know how many times I gotta tell yo' ass that. Stop havin' such a nasty attitude and work with me." He'd been spitting the same lines since he'd brought me there, and now I was hardly moved by how sweet it sounded. I was bored and irritable from trying to eat healthy and the lack of sex in my life didn't help my mood any either. As if he'd read my mind, his brows rose. "You want some dick? That's why you're actin' up?"

I hated how cocky he was and even though I really wanted to bring up Carmise, I couldn't deny the immediate reaction my body had to him. His grin grew at my silence, and he kneeled on the bed, sliding my little throw blanket off me. My mind was telling me to at least play hard to get, but my thighs were already spreading as he ran his rough hands up my legs. His touch was even more enticing than the thought of him filling me up, and my spine tingled as he laid on top of me, careful not to put weight on my belly.

"If you wanted me to fuck you, that's all you had to say, baby." Grinding his dick right at my center had me damn near cumming. The thin fabric of his pajama bottoms had me feeling everything and I bit my lip to stifle the soft ass moan I felt about to erupt. As soon as I locked my legs around him, he flipped me over so that I was on top. "Come put that pussy on my tongue," he commanded huskily, lifting my small frame over his face with ease. Trembling, I held on to the thick, quilted headboard as he pushed my panties to the side and slithered his tongue between my slippery folds.

"Ahhh." A sigh of satisfaction fell from my lips at the contact. I slowly rocked against his mouth and nose, reaching a new level of bliss each time my clit was stroked. Pregnancy had me so sensitive that I was climaxing in seconds, but Quay continued to work his tongue, sending shock waves through my body. "Quay, I-I can't take any more!" I whined, trying to move away, only for him to hold me in place. My stomach caved in as another orgasm tore through me. Finally releasing me, I fell against the bed completely spent, but Quay was far from done. He slipped out of his clothes, while I laid there panting and trying to catch my breath.

Once he was naked, he laid on top of me, sucking my lips into his mouth as his dick nudged at my opening. I'd re-energized quickly and squirmed beneath him, trying to force him to put it in, only coming close enough for only his head to slip in.

"Quit playin', Quuuuaaay! Put it innnnn!" I begged, growing more frustrated every time he came close to filling me up.

"You gone stop with that smart mouth shit?" His voice had a teasing ring to it as he sucked my neck, giving it a light nip with his teeth.

"Yes!"

"I still don't know if you deserve this dick though, you been kinda—"

"Dammit Quay, just fuck meeee!" I'd barely got the words out when he slammed into me. He brought his lips back to mine, stroking my tongue with his as he took his time rocking in and out of me with precision.

"This pussy cryin' for me, it must've missed daddy." His breathing was shaky, giving away just how good it felt to him too. I moved in sync with him, hungrily chasing my next nut as I squeezed my muscles tightly.

"Mmmmshit! Baby, I'm cummin'! I'm cummin'!" I screamed, clenching my thighs and hugging him to me.

"I'm right behind you, Ice baby, where you want this nut?" I could feel his dick throbbing as he got closer to filling me up with his seed.

"In me! Nut all in this pussy, bae!" That was all he needed to hear, and he groaned lowly, releasing at the exact same time as me. We laid there quietly catching our breaths until my stomach rumbled, sounding like a grizzly bear, and we both laughed.

"Let's go take a shower so I can feed my baby, man," he grumbled playfully, helping me out of bed. I couldn't deny that even though he got on my nerves, it felt good to not be at odds for one day. Not only had we ended the night on a good note, but I got a few orgasms, and I was going to bed full and satisfied.

"Well, everything seems to be looking good. Your blood pressure is normal, and you and baby are right on track for being thirteen weeks. Whatever you're doing keep it up, and I'll see you two again next week," Dr. Smith said, washing her hands before heading out of the room. She made sure to stop and pat Quay on the back, telling him "Good job," which had his ass cheesing extra hard.

"See, good dick and following doctor's orders was exactly what you needed," he said, helping me off of the table and to my feet. It had only been a few days since I'd let him fuck again, and somehow that one night had turned into almost any time I could get it. I fully blamed how horny I was on my pregnancy, but I didn't mind reaping the benefits.

"Whatever, don't sound so proud of yourself. This baby got me ready to hump a pillow half the time, you just happen to be a little bit harder." I smirked, only half kidding. The way his face cracked had me busting out laughing.

"You got jokes, huh? Yo' ass really gone be humpin' pillows when I put you on dick punishment." Immediately I choked on my laughter and shook my head. While I might have gotten pleasure from teasing him, I was not trying to miss out on the sleep-inducing orgasms he'd been delivering every day. "Yeah, that shit ain't funny no more, huh?" he taunted, and I rolled my eyes.

"See, I was just playin' and you had to take it there." Pushing him out of my way, I exited the room and stopped at the front desk to set my next appointment while he trailed behind me trying to backpedal. I guessed the only thing worse than my jokes was my attitude, and he clearly didn't want any of that smoke.

He was still trying to plead his case minutes later when we made it to the car, but I was distracted by my mom's name flashing across my screen. I didn't talk to my mama too much

because she was on the bitter side and I didn't like that negative energy around me. I didn't really think our relationship
was strained, but if we talked twice a month that was a lot.
Her calling me immediately caused me alarm. Pressing
accept, I put the phone to my ear and hesitated before
speaking.

"He-hello?"

"Isis, please don't tell me you done got evicted, little girl! I
done raised you better than to let your bills go!" she went right
in, and I rolled my eyes.

"No Ma, I didn't get evicted," I grumbled, feeling Quay
staring a hole in the side of my face. He could probably already
sense that shit was about to go left knowing of how fucked up
our relationship was.

"Well, why am I standing at your door and it's a whole ass
for rent sign in the window?"

"Probably because I moved in with my boyfriend a couple
weeks ago—"

"Oh hell, you must be pregnant! Didn't I tell you to have
your life together before you even thought about bringing a
child into this world?" Her voice elevated, and I was sure that
Quay had heard her from the driver's seat because he was
already reaching out for my phone.

"Actually, I am pregnant, but that's not why we moved in
together!" My outburst only had her laughing in my ear
bitterly.

"Well, I hope not, 'cause let me be the first to tell you that a
baby don't keep no man! As soon as he get bored or tired of yo'
ass he gone be on to the next bitch and you gone be stuck
struggling with a baby! I swear I thought you knew better than
to let a nigga get yo' ass pregnant without a ring!" she
continued to go off until Quay snatched my phone and hung
up on her.

"Why would you do that? She's gonna call back thinking I hung up on her!"

"So! Fuck that bitch, I ain't bouta let you get stressed out 'cause her bitter ass on the phone talkin' down on you! Naw, we not doin' that." He shook his head, dropping my phone into his lap and shutting down any argument I may have had. My mama was the last person I should've allowed to take me out of my element, but that didn't stop me from feeling some type of way about her opinion. Technically, she wasn't wrong though. Quay was hardly reliable and he stayed being distracted by other women. I could only imagine how he was going to be once I couldn't see my feet anymore or worse, when I had the baby. I shook the thoughts off, trying not to let them fuck up my mood, but it was already too late. Just that fast, she had come in like always and had me questioning my reality and preparing for the worst.

CHAPTER NINETEEN
ADORE

"She said *what*? Oh hell naw, sis, you better cut her ass off until after you have the baby! Shit, I don't even know if you should talk to her then. That was some wild ass shit to say to yo' baby." I moved around getting ready for my first meeting with the new lawyer I'd retained. My video had blown up and people were coming out of the woodwork to offer me their services. From legal advice to somebody starting a GoFundMe for me, I was at no shortage on resources. Out of all the lawyers that had reached out to me Lacy Stephen was the one I'd chosen. For one, she was a black woman, so I felt like she'd better understand what I was dealing with and fight that much harder for me. I also checked her credentials and she was the best at her firm, having never lost a case in the years she'd been practicing. She was a pit bull in a skirt and I couldn't wait to see what she type of case she'd be able to pull from the shit the Blacks had dragged me into.

"That's the same thing Quay said. He was so pissed off he hung up on her," Isis tittered, sucking her teeth. "That man ain't playin' about me stressin' his baby out."

"As he should. He better protect yo' mental health," I clowned, even though I was proud of him for stepping up. In the last few weeks he'd been on his shit when it came to taking care of Isis. Even going so far as to force me into silence about what was going on with Niko. Her being on bed rest did make it easier to keep the lie going that I was busy with work and getting Kaliyah back.

"See, don't be giving him too much credit now, that shit will go straight to his head." She tried to sound irritated but I could hear the smile in her voice. My brother was over there breaking down the walls she'd built and I was rooting for him to win her back. "How you and Heavy doin'? Y'all know y'all my couple goals, right?"

"We're doing okay for now, but we're far from couple goals. Sometimes I be wanting to go upside his head," I muttered. Since she wasn't aware that I had to stay there she didn't know how frustrating it was to be unable to leave when he got on my nerves. I couldn't lie, there could've been a worse prison. At least his house was big enough that I didn't have to see his fine ass if I didn't want to. So far we'd only had a few disagreements though. Most of the time we got along great, especially when we were both naked.

"Girl, don't play, Heavy over there wearing that thang out! Talkin' 'bout far from couple goals! Y'all the shit!"

"I'm not bouta play with you, bitch."

"That's 'cause you know I'm tellin' the truth. It's ok, you ain't gotta tell me, I can see that shit all in the glow on yo' face," she said, leaning into the camera like she needed a close up to be sure she saw what she claimed. "Yep, that's definitely a glow.'"

"Let me call you back boo, it's almost time for me to go." Her bored ass instantly pouted but didn't put up a fight as we said our goodbyes and hung up. I still had a good hour before it was time to go, so I put the finishing touches on my makeup. I went with a fresh everyday look and it matched the nude one piece I was wearing. Satisfied with my overall look, I headed downstairs and set my things on the couch so they'd be there when I finally left.

"You need a ride or you gone drive?" Heavy strolled out of the kitchen shirtless with only a pair of gray sweatpants on. True to his word, he'd been teaching me how to drive and while I got the basics, I wasn't ready to be driving around the city on my own.

"Now you know damn well." I grinned, seeing the lust in his eyes as he walked toward me. "You need to be throwing on some clothes instead of walkin' round here with those thot pants on." I immediately began backing away until I ran into the back of the couch.

"You runnin' and I was only tryna get a kiss before we go." I looked at him suspiciously as he stepped between my legs, pecking my at lips. The kiss grew heavier and I had to pull away.

"Nope, go get dressed. I don't wanna be late." I dodged his lips again, making him laugh.

"I got you, we gon' be there on time, don't even worry." The sneaky grin on his face should've told me he was on some funny shit, but it wasn't until he pulled his Ferrari Stradale out of the garage twenty minutes later that I knew for sure. I never saw him drive this car because he said it was too flashy and was an impulse buy from when he made his first million.

"Oh hell naw." I shook my head as he grinned and revved the engine. "I'm not riding in that with you."

"Come on, it's a special occasion. I promise I won't go too fast," he coaxed. Checking the time on my phone, I sighed, knowing I didn't have time to argue about it. As soon as I dropped into the butter soft seat and tightened my seatbelt around me, he was burning rubber out of the driveway. I had to admit that even though I was slightly terrified at how fast he was going, he looked sexy as hell maneuvering through traffic with one hand on the steering wheel and the other on my thigh.

I ended up being so focused on him that I didn't even realize we were at Lacy's office. After finding a spot in the parking garage, he walked with me into the building with my hand wrapped in his. Suddenly I was nervous, even though just that morning I'd been hopeful, and Heavy noticed, giving my hand a reassuring squeeze.

"Aye, you got this. If this one don't got nothin' for us then we'll move on to the next," he promised softly, and I relaxed just a little bit more. We'd made it with ten minutes to spare thanks to Heavy's crazy driving, so the secretary was calling me back in no time. Heavy tried to release my hand, but I held it tightly, prompting him to come with me. He'd been too much of a support system for me to not have him close.

"Hey Adore, it's so nice to finally meet you!" Lacy gushed, reaching to shake my hand, and I was momentarily stunned at how much more beautiful she was in person. She was a whole black Barbie in real life.

"It's really nice to meet you too. This is my boyfriend, Dominique." Still smiling, she shook his hand also before guiding us over to a couple of chairs in front of her desk.

"Well, let me get right to it. Now after studying your contract, I noticed a few things. One, you were under eighteen when you signed the contract, which I'm sure you weren't accompanied by your mother when you did, and that's an angle to fight this thing. Next, being a pregnant minor that was imprisoned at the time of signing can also be considered duress. You already had been sentenced and was made to believe signing the contract was in your best interest, which we all know it was not." My heartbeat quickened in excitement. "Niko will probably go after you for breaking the contract by outing them online, so we'll get that thrown out first and then we'll work on custody, which should be even easier considering how ridiculous the stipulations are. I could certainly get you visitation to start with and either joint custody or full custody since you were also a victim of the son."

She was still talking and informing me of my options while I blinked back tears of joy. When she finished, I looked at Heavy to see if he felt like it was a good idea. Just the expression on his face let me know he liked everything she was saying just like I did, and I quickly agreed for her to get the ball rolling.

I ended up leaving feeling much more optimistic, and even though my first instinct was to inform the people on TikTok that had been asking for an update, Lacy had advised against posting any of the things we discussed just to protect our plan of attack from Niko or anybody he associated with. That was fine with me since I didn't want anything getting in the way of me getting my baby back.

"You hungry?" Heavy asked once we had left the office, and my stomach instantly growled. I'd skipped breakfast because I was too excited to eat but now since it was over and everything looked good, I was ready to pig out.

"Oh my god, hell yeah! My stomach been in my back for a minute!" I admitted, thinking of what I might have a taste for.

"Ayite, I was thinking Ruth's Chris, but if you want something else then—"

"Something else over a steak? You should already know what," I said, and we both laughed as he took a detour. Just thinking about a juicy steak had my toes curling in my shoes.

"Greedy ass," he eyed me and said, but I only shrugged, completely unbothered by the insult. We arrived shortly after that and I could already smell the aroma of food on the outside of the building. Heavy slipped the hostess a couple of bills and bypassed any wait for a table.

"I want the most expensive champagne you got," he requested once we were seated, and I lifted my brows in surprise. I rarely ever saw him drink so I knew he was in a good ass mood. The server immediately brought the bottle over to us and poured us two pretty tall flutes. "To you, amazing me again by your determination. I'm proud of you, baby. You're out here making big moves and I'm just happy to be a part of it."

"Awwww! Thank you, baby!" I tapped his glass with mine and took a healthy sip. It felt good to finally have things going my way for real, and I knew a big part of that blessing was Heavy. Ever since I'd met him he'd been like good luck for me because all of the bad things that happened turned out to have an even better outcome. I was truly grateful that I had given him a chance.

CHAPTER TWENTY

HEAVY

I t had been a minute since I'd spent the day with my baby girl and I decided to drop in on her. It was one of the few free days she had where she wasn't at any practices or hanging with her little friends. The need to see her had been spur of the moment though, so it was really going to be a surprise for her for real. I pulled into their driveway behind Sha'ron's car and prayed that she kept the same energy she'd been having with me. I made the short trip to the door and frowned at the sound of loud ass music coming from inside as I rang the bell. After waiting a few, I realized she couldn't hear it over the speakers inside, so I called her phone and it immediately went to voicemail. Fed up, I called Kay Kay's phone, pissed that I was about to have her answer the door when it was usually a rule that she didn't, even if she knew it was me.

"Hey Daddy!" she gushed, cheesing into the phone. I could see her dolls in the background so I knew she was at least in her room away from whatever her mama had going on, which put me at ease a little.

"Hey baby, come open the door. I came to pick you up but

yo' mama must can't hear the bell over the music." I tried to keep the irritation out of my voice, but someone in the background whispering had my face balled up tight. "Yo, who is that?"

"Those my play cousins, Ayanna and Ashland. They're nosy," she whispered the last part as she moved around, clearly coming to let me in. The music grew louder as she neared the front of the house. I tried to listen and see if I could hear anything besides the deafening bass, but I could only make out muffled voices in the background. A second later the locks were turning, and my baby stood on the other side with her hair all over her head.

"Go get yo' iPad and stuff, baby, I'ma go holla at yo' mama." She took off to her room while I went in search of Sha'ron and found her in the living room with two other women. Liquor bottles were scattered all over the coffee table as they sat around trying to console my distraught baby mama. I went completely unnoticed until I came further in the room and turned the music off.

"What the fuck you doin, Ronnie? Yo' ass gettin' drunk while Kay Kay here?" I questioned, trying to resist the urge to yank her ass.

"Damn girl, yo' baby daddy just be walkin' in yo' crib like he own the place?" one of the girls scoffed even as she eyed me lustfully. Ignoring her, I put my attention back on Sha'ron, who had her head resting in the other girl's lap but quickly sat up, waving her finger at me.

"Don't start, Dominique! This shit is your fault anyway! How the hell you even get in here?" she slurred, blinking rapidly. It was obvious they'd been drinking for a while and the shit had hit her much harder than the others.

"It don't matter who let me in! Yo' ass in here too drunk to answer the shit yourself any-mufuckin-way!" Sighing, I brushed a hand down my waves and snapped my fingers at her two random ass friends. "Aye, tweedle-dee and tweedle-dum, y'all ass gotta go. Grab yo' shit and yo' kids and take y'all asses on somewhere."

"We don't gotta go nowhere, Sha'ron invited us here!" the first one said, rolling her neck while the other frowned up her nose at me.

"Ugh, Ronnie, you got one of them baby daddies that think they own you. I'm glad Quan and Rex know better than to come in my shit making demands." I could see my baby mama taking in the shit they were saying like her situation was anything like theirs. I was almost positive that neither of shorty's baby daddies were active with her kids, and they damn sure weren't paying the bills at her house, which should've made their points null and void, but drunk minds didn't have logic. They were still rambling when I pulled my gun off my waist, but they instantly grew silent when they heard my safety click. They're eyes almost popped out of their heads, and while one ran out the door the other ran to Kay Kay's room to retrieve her kids. Putting the safety back on, I tucked my gun back away so the two little girls wouldn't see it, when Sha'ron ran up on me swinging.

"I hate you! I hate you! You're always taking something from me! Why couldn't you just leave Bronx alone!" Holding her by the arms, I shoved her crazy ass off me, completely confused by her sudden rage over Bronx's dead ass. I didn't know what she thought I'd say to that, but I damn sure wasn't about to admit to shit.

"Ronnie, bro, you better go lay down and sleep this shit off. My fuckin' baby in here and I ain't tryna have her see you actin' a fool!" I said through clenched teeth.

"Ha! You sure she's yours? Is that why you killed Bronx, 'cause you know he's probably really her daddy!" Hearing a gasp from across the room, I saw my baby peeking around the corner with tears in her eyes and I wanted to punch Sha'ron's teeth down her throat. Her drunk ass blinked like she was surprised to see my baby right there before she began bawling again.

"Hey, come here, baby. Come to Daddy." Turning my back to Sha'ron's goofy ass, I crouched down and beckoned Kay Kay to me. Seeing the mixture of emotions on her face felt like my heart was being ripped from my chest. She was supposed to remain clueless about anything pertaining to Bronx, and it figured her mama would be the one to let it slip on some bitter shit. As mad as I was, I forced a smile to put her at ease, and after a bit of reassurance she finally came from behind the wall. She walked over to me slowly as fat tears landed on her cheeks until she finally reached my outstretched arms.

"Was Uncle Bronx really my daddy?" she asked, wrapping her arms around my neck tightly.

"Nope, you're all me, Kay Kay. I'm the one that made you, the one that cut yo' umbilical cord, the first one that held you, and I named you. You're all mine, baby girl. You understand?" I didn't even realize I was crying until I tasted a salty tear, and I hurried to wipe my face as I lifted her off her feet. She still had her face hidden away, but I felt her nodding as I sent a warning glare Sha'ron's way. She'd fucked up putting our daughter in this shit and judging from the pitiful look on her face, she knew it. I didn't feel an ounce of sympathy for her and I wasn't going to explain away the fuck shit she'd just done. Thankfully, for the time being, Kay Kay seemed content with my answer. She remained quiet as I carried her out to my truck, but after a while she hummed my name again.

"Yes, baby?" I glanced at her in the rearview, noting the serious expression on her face.

"What's a ambililcal cord?" I sighed in relief that she

wasn't trying to ask more questions and chuckled at her mispronouncing the word.

"It's how yo' mama shares food with you when you're in her belly." I gave the simplest version I could, only for her to have five more questions for each answer. It was much easier to explain babies to her than it was to explain her mama's bullshit. By the time I pulled up at home she was in a much better mood.

Adore being inside and offering to have a girl's night so she could do her hair was the icing on the cake. I sent her to take a shower first and while she was upstairs, I snuck up behind Adore in the kitchen as she prepared snacks for them. "I thought you ain't know how to do hair?" I quizzed, giving her a knowing look as she shrugged.

"I mean, I'm not a pro, but I can do a couple ponytails." Her voice trailed off with the lie and I could tell she was self-conscious about it. Stifling a laugh, I stole some of the popcorn she was pouring and gained an elbow in my rib.

"I'ma just help you so yo' ass don't have my baby round here with crooked parts and loose ponytails." Her neck instantly snapped backwards and she looked up at me, impressed.

"*You* know how to do hair?"

Mocking her, I jumped my shoulders nonchalantly. "I mean, I ain't a pro, but I know how to do the basics." Feigning an attitude, she shook me off, but I didn't release my arms from her waist. "My bad, I'm just fuckin' with you, man."

"It's not funny, Dominique!"

"Nah, it's not, especially when you're a girl mom, but I'ma hook you up, watch," I promised pressing a kiss behind her ear, and she shuddered like she always did from my affection. An hour later we were in the living room watching *Encanto* again. Kay Kay sat crossed leg on the floor in front of Adore while I

instructed her on how to make a straight part and secure ponytails. She had her lip tucked between her teeth in deep concen-
tration, and I knew it didn't help that Kay Kay was a wiggle
worm, especially when her favorite movie was on. I had to
admit she did a decent job despite how loose the hair ties were.
When she finally let my baby up I held back a laugh.

"You like it, Daddy?" She jumped around, shaking the few
barrettes that were on the ends so that they clinked together
noisily.

"Mmhmm!" Nodding, I gave her a forced hum that she was
too busy bouncing to notice, but once she did I already knew
she was going to hurt Adore's feelings. She was already looking
at her proudly until she noticed my reaction and threw a
pillow at me, which started a whole pillow fight with me
against them. I made sure to rock Kay Kay's head every time
too so when we all finally fell out exhausted, those loose ass
braids had rubbed out.

CHAPTER TWENTY-ONE

QUAY

I stepped through the door of Hector's warehouse and shot Heavy an irritated look when two beefy ass niggas began frisking us. The one searching me immediately began speaking in Spanish all fast when he found a knife against my ankle.

"Didn't I tell yo' ass no weapons?" he had the nerve to say, mugging me as they tossed my shit on a desk behind them.

"You said no guns, it's a difference," I grumbled as they finished searching me. "Aye, I want that back when I leave too." I pointed so he could somewhat understand what I said, because I was serious about getting my shit back. Scoffing, Heavy grabbed the bags of money, tossing me one as we headed deeper into the warehouse. I followed his lead since this was my first time meeting Hector, and the little fat man behind the desk was the last thing I was expecting. When he saw us he stood, smiling widely, and I didn't blame him. He had damn near a million reasons to smile seeing us.

"Hey brother, it's been a long time!" he said, shaking Heavy's hand before turning to me. "And who do we have here?" Stepping back, he sized me up before sticking his hand out to me.

"This is my new partner, Quay. Quay, this is Hector." Heavy gave a quick introduction and I gripped his little hand firmly. Snapping his fingers, a couple of niggas with AKs strapped on their chests stepped forward, and I handed my bag over like Heavy had done.

"Sit down, fellas. It's going to take a few minutes to count and load you up," Hector said, moving back behind the desk. "You look familiar. Have we done business before?" His eyes narrowed on me trying to place my face, and I immediately shook my head. I knew damn well I'd never seen his ass a day in my life.

"Naw, it wasn't me."

"You sure?" he asked again, making my jaw clench this time to keep from saying something I'd regret. It was only my first time meeting the connect as a partner and I wasn't trying to fuck shit up for Heavy, but I also wasn't about to keep repeating myself. "Ohhh, now I know where I've seen you before. You and your sister share similar features. Adore, right?" His eyes lit up as they bounced to Heavy, who nodded, while I leaned to the edge of my seat.

"How the fuck you know my sister?" I frowned, looking between him and Heavy. There was no way his ass had been goofy enough to introduce his ass to anyone close to him. Heavy opened his mouth, but one flip of the hand from Hector and he shut that shit right up.

"You don't think I'd allow you here without doing my research, right?" He laughed and his non-English speaking men did as well, like they knew exactly what was being said. I didn't find the joke and it irritated me that he did all that just to let me know he'd done his research on me. "I know every-thing about each of you from your mother to your pregnant girlfriend, Isis. No need to worry though, I only like to know who I'm dealing with and from what I've seen, you're a much better fit than Bronx. I like that you're, *como se' dice?* Uh, blunt. I think we have that in common." His smile was friendly like he hadn't just slickly threatened my family, and I immediately realized I hated his ass.

"You're good, man." Heavy grabbed my shoulder, giving it a light squeeze to let me know to chill.

"I may have also seen Miss Adore's face slide across my desk recently." Hector leaned forward speaking lowly, and Heavy instantly perked up.

"And where did it go?"

"You know I can't say, but I may be able to set something up for you to... redirect." He shrugged casually and I almost lunged for his throat, but Heavy's massive hand dropped back on my shoulder.

"Do that ASAP. I'll even throw in something extra." He stood, seeing the workers coming back our way with four duffels.

"I'll see what I can do," the greedy ass nigga was quick to say at the promise of extra money. For appearances sake, I shook the man's hand just like Heavy did before we carried the bags out to the truck.

Once we finished distributing the keys to the different houses, I went to see the nigga Manny. The shit Rock had told me was weighing on me heavy and I didn't like not addressing that shit. Since I finally had some free time in my schedule, I was going to ride down on him and see if I could get through to his ass before I had to make him disappear. Pulling up at his main girl's crib on Blackstone, I tucked my gun in my jeans and walked up the concrete steps, hitting the buzzer. He was expecting me, so the door immediately unlocked, and I took the stairs to the second floor. As soon as I got to her apartment door I could hear a bunch of shit going on inside, pissing me off. I'd been told him I was coming, so any company he had in that bitch should've left long before I arrived.

A second later his girl opened the door in some small ass silk shorts and a matching sports bra, smoking a blunt. I immediately turned up my nose at the stale scent that damn near choked me as her kids ran from one room to another.

"He in the front." She waved dismissively toward her living room where the sound of music and a gang of niggas was coming from. All eyes were on me when I hit the open door-way, and I counted about five niggas sitting around smoking one blunt.

"What's up, bro?" Manny said, giving me a head nod, immediately putting his attention back on the TV screen. My jaw clenched at the disrespect, but I decided to let the shit slide, noting that he was just about out of chances with me.

"Come holla at me." There was no doubt that it was more of a command than a request and everybody in there knew it. They all looked his way to see what he would do, and just like I expected, he stood his ass up and followed me out into the hallway.

"What's up man, I was in the middle of somethin'." He shuffled agitatedly from one foot to the other, and I looked at his ass in disgust. The dingy ass clothes he had on were probably two or three days old and his face looked more scruffy than usual.

"Sittin' around watchin' TV and sharin' a blunt with a room full of niggas ain't being in the middle of shit!" His head snapped in my direction, and he grit his teeth.

"Well, what the fuck else I'm supposed to do since you

suspended me, *boss!*" he spat, puffing up his chest. His little attitude had me laughing on the inside, because I was sure he
didn't expect me to give a fuck about that slick ass comment.

"You right, I *am* yo' boss! Nigga, I been yo' boss and Heavy
or nan other nigga done changed a fuckin' thing! I expected
you to get on yo' shit, but it's obvious you tryna throw some lil'
hoe ass pity party. And if that's what you wanna do, that's cool.
We ain't gotta be shit to each other if that's what you want.
But if I find out you out here movin' grimy and speakin' ill on
my name, you ain't gone have to worry about havin' a boss or
shit else! Feel me?" By now I was so close to him I could smell
his musty ass pits, but I needed to get my point across, so he
knew just how serious I was. His nostrils flared as he looked
straight ahead, past me, and focused on the wall, tightening
his crusty ass lips but knowing better than to get buck with
me. Satisfied that I'd gotten my point across, I shoulder
checked his ass on my way out the building.

I hadn't ever given his ass a reason to feel like I thought I
was better than him or any other nigga on my team. If need be,
I'd still get on the block, still bag up, still ride down on any
nigga, 'cause I was a real one. Taking the position with Heavy
was a money move that anyone in their right mind would've
taken and ran with, and I couldn't understand how the fuck his
tender dick ass couldn't see that shit. It didn't really matter
though, because I had family to be worried about, and that
didn't include no grown ass nigga that couldn't even wash his
ass on a daily basis.

Sighing heavily, I hopped back in my car and gave his
building one last look, hoping his ass took heed to my words.
He was a day one and I fucked with him, but I wasn't above
taking out a nigga before they came for me.

CHAPTER TWENTY-TWO

ISIS

I blew out an aggravated breath and plopped back against the couch as my tenth call to Quay went unanswered. His ass always managed to froggy leap to answer any call he got while he was in the house, but as soon as he left, he acted like he couldn't use his fingers. He'd promised to take me to my store so I could check my inventory and set up an online store until I had his big-headed baby, but I hadn't talked to him in hours. If he didn't do this shit consistently, then I probably would've thought something was wrong, but that was never the case. He either had his phone off or was screening his calls, which really pissed me off because I was at home alone during a high-risk pregnancy. All I wanted was to have something productive to do with my time besides watch TV and eat snacks, but he couldn't even come through to help me with that.

Trying him one last time and getting the same results, I shuffled to my room and snatched up the other set to my keys. He thought all this time that he had been stopping me when really, I'd just been trying to do right on my own. After seeing how hurt he was about the abortion and me almost having a miscarriage, I was trying to take it easy, but I also wasn't about to lose my business because of his ass. Making sure I had all my stuff, I slipped on my UGG boots and coat before going out to the garage where my baby was warming up. The weather was so up and down that I never knew what to expect, but I wasn't going to be caught slipping without some type of heat because the way the wind was set up, it would blow straight through my little winter coat.

Thankfully, by the time I got behind the wheel everything was nice and warm. I took my time finding the right song in Apple music and cut it all the way up as I pulled out. It felt so good being able to take myself somewhere and listening to what I wanted to listen to. Quay hated anything that had to do with Meg or the City Girls, so it never got any play in his shit on our weekly doctor trips. Feeling free, I bopped in my seat and rapped every lyric word for word before I pulled up at my dark ass, empty store. It had been a minute since I'd even seen it and I hated that amongst the other stores on the block my shit looked shut down.

Sucking my teeth, I tried to tell myself that it was only temporary as I hurried to the door trying to beat the cold. Having the heat off for so long had the inside colder than the outside, and I hurried to adjust the thermostat and cut on the light before making my way to the back. There were still boxes and boxes of unopened items in the storage room and all of it was winter stuff. It irritated me that Quay wasn't there to move shit around like I needed to because I wasn't stupid enough to be trying to lift any of that shit by myself.

I was still standing in the middle of the storage room looking crazy a few minutes later, when heavy knocking had me clutching my chest. When I finally calmed down, I went to peek from behind the storage room door to the front window.

My forehead bunched seeing two girls standing in the doorway bouncing around trying to keep warm. I immediately noticed that they didn't seem like they were just trying to get in out of the cold, judging from the many bags they each carried. Curiously, I made my way to the door and they both started asking if I was open, even though my store sign was off.

"I'm closed!" I shouted, hoping they heard me through the glass, and they must have because the disappointment was evident.

"Please, I'm only looking for one thing!" the one in a purple puffer coat put her hands together begging. I immediately contemplated if I should let this money slip through my fingers and decided that it would be stupid. She said she only needed one thing and that should've only taken a few minutes, so my thirsty ass opened the door. They both shimmied inside, eyes lighting up at the things on my shelves.

"Look, I'm really not open so y'all gone have to make this quick," I let them know, and they instantly began picking up items that definitely went over her one thing promise. I wasn't even tripping though, it was more money for me and my baby.

"Girl, when did you open back up? I could've sworn I passed here a little while ago and y'all was closed, lights off and everything. I thought you was closed for good. I was salty as hell 'cause you stay with a good deal." The girl dressed in all black was now talking as she piled a couple things in her arms.

"Naw, I'm actually about to only do online sells until I have my baby because my doctor got me on light duty."

"Damn, babies always gettin' in the way of a bag." Purple coat shook her head and tsked.

"I swear, that's why I love that my mama watches mine whenever I need her to, 'cause I got money to make. I can't be just laying around broke waiting on a nigga to take care of me,"

Ms. All Black said, sticking her tongue out and slapping fives with her friend.

"I know that's right! Them lil' muhfuckas need to eat then I need to make money!" They went off on a whole tangent about the expenses of raising a child while I got lost in my thoughts once again. It was the second time I'd been advised to make my money and I was hearing the message loud and clear.

"Okay, we ready now!" they said loudly, snapping me out of my thoughts as they piled their armfuls of stuff on the counter. I began ringing them up and got giddy just seeing their total rise higher and higher.

Once I had them each bagged up and on their way, I counted out the seven hundred dollars I had just made in less than twenty minutes and did a little dance. I'd forgotten how exciting it was to actually make money, and I realized that I was missing out on a lot just to sit and bake a baby. Knowing that I didn't have anything to go back to, I decided to stick around the store for a little bit longer. Quay rarely ever got home before ten and it wouldn't hurt to be productive and make some money since I was already breaking the rules. I went to shut on the open sign and almost immediately, customers began coming in like I had a special sale going on. A lot of the things on the floor were midseason items, but that didn't stop them from racking up, which worked out perfect for me since I wouldn't have to move clothes twice. Despite me going against his wishes, I was sure that Quay would be proud that I'd figured out a way to get work done without having to do any real work. I didn't even have to stand up because I eventually pulled out the swivel stool from the back room.

I ended up spending about five hours at the store before deciding to close up shop and go home. Even though it seemed like I hadn't done much, I was beat by the time I parked my car in the garage and dragged myself into the house. Luckily, no one was there when I returned and I was able to take a quick shower and hop right back in my bed. Getting comfortable, I watched Netflix and made plans to do the same thing the next day as soon as Quay strolled his lanky ass out the door in the morning.

CHAPTER TWENTY-THREE
ADORE

"Oooh, that's cute!" Isis gushed, pointing out a light blue, two-piece pantsuit, and I immediately frowned.

"Not for court though," I said, still putting it in my cart even though I needed something a bit more presentable, considering this would be my first appearance before a judge. Lacy had managed to get me a court date in three weeks. It seemed like the ball was rolling way faster than I'd expected and I was almost too excited to function. I didn't want to take any chances on my court clothes not coming in time, so I was ordering them early and putting a rush on delivery.

"True," she admitted. "I hope the doctor gives me the okay to come to court with you though. I want you to have as much support in there as possible 'cause ain't no tellin' who those miserable bitches gone try to bring." Rolling her eyes, she turned over on her side and propped her head up, getting more comfortable. We still hadn't told her about Niko's threat on my life, and her mentioning them instantly put it in the forefront of my mind. Being in a courtroom with a judge and a bunch of members of the law had put me at ease so that I wasn't really thinking about it too much, but I couldn't deny how slippery they were. Heavy had already promised to be by my side the entire time and that made me feel a whole lot better. He'd already been doing everything he could to keep us safe, so knowing he'd be right there took a weight off my shoulders, especially considering that Niko was afraid of him. The thought of how he'd bitched up both times he was in Heavy's presence brought a grin to my face. "Oooh, this the one, bitch!" Isis's loud ass snapped me out of my thoughts, pointing to a black pinstripe suit that ruffled around the legs and sleeves. I could already see myself strolling into the courtroom in it looking like a whole professional.

"Yessssss, that one *is* nice," I agreed, quickly putting it in my cart also. Heavy had given me his credit card and told me to get everything I would need for all of the times we'd be appearing before a judge, and I was already burning a hole in it with the assistance of Isis. "Okay, that's it. I already got a couple thousand in this cart thanks to you," I scolded, going to the checkout page, and she sat up, palming her chest.

"Don't try to put that shit off on me! You're the one dropping shit that you know you're not even going to wear to court in your cart! It really don't matter anyway 'cause when a nigga with money gives you his card, that means go crazy." She shrugged.

"That is not what that means, fool."

"The lies! Any time Quay run me his card, it ain't no limit. Did he tell you to only spend a certain amount?" She blinked, already knowing that he hadn't, and when I didn't say anything she gave me a pointed look. "Exactly! No limit!" I rolled my eyes at her goofy ass as she started humming Usher's song, "No Limit."

Once I was finished with my shopping, I closed her laptop

and got comfortable. Isis had turned on *Harlem* and I didn't want to miss any of the drama. I loved me some Megan Goode, and without a doubt she was my favorite character. By the time Heavy and Quay returned from whatever run they were going to make I was going to have finished the whole season. They'd already been gone for a few hours and even Isis had said that my brother was always out late. I didn't have to work the next day so it didn't matter to me, I just didn't want their asses to come right in the middle of an episode. At some point after episode four I fell asleep, only to be woken up by Heavy lifting me out of a sleeping Isis's bed.

"Hey," I cooed, kissing his exposed neck as he carried me from the room quietly.

"It's crazy you sound like the grumpy old troll when you sleep and sound like a mouse when yo' ass is woke," he cracked, and I slapped him in the chest with an eyeroll.

"I don't sound like either of those. And I called myself tryna be sweet to you."

"Awwww, you sad now? I'm sorry, bae. I love yo' loud ass snore and yo' mousy voice." He leaned down trying to kiss me and I avoided his lips entirely, giving him my cheek.

"Nope, no kisses for you."

He laughed at me folding my arms petulantly and gave a quick, "Yeah ayite." I didn't know what he thought, but I could definitely hold a grudge, or at least I'd try to anyway. The longest I'd been able to be mad at him was almost a few hours, but he came back being all cute and charming, immediately breaking down my walls. Once we got to the bottom of the stairs I wiggled out of his arms. Laughing, he watched me slip into my shoes and coat, before handing me my backpack purse that I'd forgotten about. I snatched it out of his hand and rolled my eyes, stomping out the door ahead of him.

By the time we made it home, I'd beat my own record and

no longer had an attitude once Heavy ate my pussy and fucked me into a coma. I was sure he already had it planned judging from the cocky smirk on his face as he made me apologize with each stroke, until I felt couldn't take anymore and fell asleep in the fetal position just like I knew his ass wanted.

CHAPTER TWENTY-FOUR
HEAVY

It was a week before Adore's first court date and I could tell that the closer we got the more worried she became of what the outcome might be. Aside from keeping a close eye on her, I still had yet to get Hector to set up the meet with Black's hitman and I was starting to think he was doing the shit on purpose. Shit was really starting to make me look at him funny, but until he actually did something to cross me I wouldn't jump the gun.

I was in the middle of trying to get sleep, when my phone started jumping with back-to-back messages. Seeing Sha'ron's name instantly had me ready to cut the shit off. I still had Kay Kay since the day she'd let that goofy shit roll off her tongue in front of her, and I had no intentions on taking her back any time soon. It hurt to see her going down such a spiral, but I wasn't going to help her until she decided that she wanted the help. Reading the messages, I jumped up, careful not to wake Adore as I scrambled to throw on some sweats. Even as crazy as she had sounded the last time I saw her, I hadn't been too concerned, but the shit she'd just sent my phone had me on high alert.

I slipped out of the house quietly and jumped in my truck, grateful that she didn't live too far away. The whole way there I told myself that I was being goofy for even trying to help her ass as I dialed her phone back-to-back with no answer. "Fuck!" I shouted, pounding my fist on the steering wheel. It felt like everybody was out slowing me down when really it was only a few cars on the road. By the time I reached her block I was already pulling off my seatbelt so I could hop straight out, and that's exactly what I did, damn near wrecking her car as I pulled into her driveway. Just like the last time I was there the radio was up loud as hell and, of course, the door was locked tight.

"Ronnie! Ronnie!" I shouted, kicking her door with force until it finally flew open, and the sight before me had my mind racing. Her apartment was tore the fuck up. There was glass and shit everywhere like a tornado had flown through, or somebody that was pissed off, which only had me more frantic. I checked every room on the first floor and came up empty, giving me a little bit of hope, but the second I stepped on the landing at the top of the stairs my chest deflated. There was literally blood from the top of the stairs to the master bedroom smeared into the cream carpet. It looked like a horror movie, and despite the shit I'd done to niggas in the past, knowing that it was a good chance I was seeing my baby mama's blood had me sick. Against my better judgment, I followed the trail until I came to her body on the floor. Running over to her, I dropped down and cradled her bloody head. She was covered in scratches and bruises on every inch of her exposed skin.

"What the fuck, Ronnie! Hey, hey, wake up!" I shouted, slapping her cheek as she laid limply in my arms. It took me a few minutes to realize there was no way she'd done this to herself. My mind raced trying to think of who would've done some shit like that to her, and I drew a big ass blank. The sound of sirens gave me hope that maybe she could still be helped, and I gently laid her head back down so I could let them in. They stayed in a quiet neighborhood, so I was sure one of her nosy ass neighbors had heard what happened and called the police. I made it down the stairs just as they kicked the door in. "She's upstairs—"

"Put your hands up and get on the floor!" A rush of officers stormed inside, pointing guns and flashlights in my face, momentarily stunning me as I tried to tell them where Sha'ron was. "I said put your fuckin' hands up!"

"Look my baby mama upstairs, somebody—"

"Shut the fuck up!" Before I could get another word out I was kicked in the leg, making me kneel as at least ten officers swarmed me, barking different orders. Not trying to get shot, I raised my bloody hands up like they said and realized I must have looked like the person who'd come in and attacked Sha'ron. As one of the officers cuffed my hands behind my head, I noticed that none of them had even gone upstairs to check on my baby mama, and I was pissed. They struggled to get me out the door as I continued to scream for somebody to get her. It seemed like every neighbor she had was standing outside watching as they shoved me in a squad car and carted my ass off to the police station.

I didn't know how much time had passed when the door to the interrogation room opened and two detectives shuffled in looking like they'd slept in their clothes. They were both white and looking at me with steely glares, and I assumed that was because of the dried blood covering my hands and arms. Goofy asses hadn't even given me a chance to clean myself up or shit. I watched them silently drop into the chairs across from me and folded my hands on top of the steel table.

"You ready to talk, *Dominique*?" the younger of the two asked. He looked like he'd just gotten out of training with his bare face and curly blond hair, and I instantly pegged him as the "good cop" with a smirk.

"Aye, I don't like the way his ass sayin' my name. Send somebody else," I said dryly, and he shot his partner a questioning look. His ass hadn't even mastered a poker face yet. The older one who proved to be the "bad cop" slammed his hand down on the table.

"Cut the shit! Why did you kill Sharon?" he roared, leaning over and hovering in my face.

"I told you I ain't touch Sha'ron. I got text messages from her saying she was about to end it and some other crazy shit so—"

"So, you decided to go over there and help her out?" he probed.

"Look, you lucky I'm even willin' to talk to y'all goofy asses. I told you what the fuck happened and I ain't sayin' shit else till my lawyer get here." I was done playing with them. They weren't trying to find out what happened anyway, they were trying to get my black ass to confess. He stared at me silently for a few seconds to intimidate me, but I was far from the weak ass niggas that shit usually worked on. I stared right back at his ass until he finally looked away, standing abruptly with his partner following right behind him. Sighing, I leaned back in my seat knowing they didn't have shit on me, but still being pissed by the inconvenience. My biggest issue was finding out how the fuck Sha'ron had gotten killed and who had the balls to do it.

The sound of the door squeaking open again snatched my attention away from my bloodstained hands, and I smirked at the sight of the mayor as he walked in looking smug.

"You had to come see for yourself, or you just bored as hell since you been fired?"

"Suspended, *temporarily*," he corrected, and my grinned widened. If no one else could be considered delusional, it was definitely him and his lame ass son. "But yes, I came to see my handywork for myself." This time it was his turn to grin as I realized what he was saying. "Smart, huh? You don't have to say it, I know."

"If it was so smart, then how the fuck you figure they gone be able to hold me for this bullshit ass charge! I can prove I wasn't nowhere around when that shit happened!" I growled, knowing that the only reason he was this close and talking this much shit was because of our location. Outside those walls, he would never be so bold.

"Ahhh, but I don't need them to hold you forever, just long enough to make my problem go away, and then I don't give a shit what you do." Shrugging, he released a supervillain laugh. "Next time, try a less worthy opponent than your father, son. I win every time," he cackled, strolling out the room.

To Be Continued...

ALSO BY J. DOMINIQUE

Made in the USA
Middletown, DE
29 August 2024